LARRY FRANCIS

I0554330

HETERONYMOUS
BOSH

Time & Place Prize Publishing
Chicago

Copyright © 2014 by Larry Francis

Author photo Copyright © 2013 M.T. O'Connor

Text set in Garamond

A Time & Place Prize Publication
Chicago

ISBN — 13: 978-0-61-588717-3

For Howard and Jacqueline

HETERONYMOUS

BOSH

Ψ

FERNANDO ANTONIA NOGUEIRA Pessoa was born in
Lisbon, Portugal in 1888. His father died when he was
five years-old. Pessoa was a poet, a writer, and a
philosopher. He is regarded as the inventor of the
heteronym in literature. Heteronyms are 'imagined'
authors with distinct, detailed physiognomies, experiences, education, friendships, families, philosophies,
and writing styles. Heteronyms are others. A heteronym exists in its own, independent world, separate
from its creator. It is estimated that Pessoa 'imagined'
more than seventy-five distinct heteronyms.

Fernando Pessoa died alone in his tidy Lisbon
apartment in 1935 at the age of forty-seven. Only after
his death was he recognized as the greatest Portuguese
poet of all time and one of the world's most significant
modernist thinkers and writers.

Hugh Everett III was born in 1930 in Washington,
D.C. He was five years-old when Fernando Pessoa
died. Everett was an American physicist, mathe-
matician, and businessman. In 1957, in his Ph.D.
dissertation, Everett proposed the idea of the relative
state formulation of quantum mechanics, which later
became known as the Many Worlds interpretation

(MWI). MWI states that the wavefunction (Ψ) is universal, which means all quantum states are realized, i.e., all possible alternative histories and futures are real. In short, *everything* and *everyone* that can exist, does exist—somewhere. And each somewhere is a discrete, parallel, actual world.

Hugh Everett died of a sudden heart attack in McLean, Virginia in 1982 at the age of fifty-one. Two generations later, his groundbreaking theory of MWI was at last recognized and embraced.

Jerome Owen Bosh was born in Chicago, Illinois in 1962. He was five years-old when Hugh Everett III published his Ph.D. dissertation and he first read Fernando Pessoa's *Book of Disquiet* when he was a twenty-one year-old university student. By breathing new life into Pessoa's and Everett's seminal ideas, Jerome Bosh rewrote our understanding of human nature and the universe.

Ψ

BLACK AND WHITE and gray. Light, then dark, then light. Images move in a big brown box. Bodies pass between. Light, then dark, then light. Flat gray shapes. A little boy. White horses pull a long wagon with big wheels draped with a giant flag. Everyone is silent. No one sees me behind the bars. Light, then dark, then light. They watch the little boy. And the horses. And the wagon. And the flag. Light, then dark, then light.

My aunt says that they are outside. The car is here. They are coming up. They are on their way in. My mommy and daddy are back home with my new baby sister. My aunt says that my sister's name is Susan. Isn't that a pretty name? Everyone loves her. She is ugly and small and loud. My aunt takes our picture. To capture the moment, she says.

Tall walls of cold white. A maze. My mommy's gloved hands. White mountains all around. It snowed for a whole day. I see my breath. My sister falls down into the soft snow. She cannot get up. She cries. I fall. I cannot get up. I cry. Mommy picks us up and brushes off the snow. She laughs and calls us her little turtles. Under a sky without color we take the snow tunnels to

5

the store. We need milk, she says. We need bread. She calls them life's staples.

The birds look like parrots to me. Small noisy parrots. There are eight of them in all. They are mostly green, but there's red, blue and yellow mixed-in too. They are all together high up in the giant elm tree in front of our apartment. The tree is sick, dying from some disease. I watch the eight parrots from the big window. Later I tell my mother about the parrots, but she does not believe me. There are no parrots in Chicago, she says, except at the zoo. They were parrots, I say. Eight parrots. I know what I saw, I say. Maybe they escaped from the zoo.

Our new house far from the city smells like paint. There's no furniture. The floors have carpet on them. Susan and I each have our own bedroom. My mom says, won't it be nice not to have to climb up stairs to get home. But I like climbing stairs. There's a backyard without a garage. All the other houses on the block have garages. There are two trees in the backyard though: an apple tree and a pear tree. Everyone can see into our backyard because there's no fence. I like our old house better. I will miss the stairs and the big window and the lilac bush next to the garage. Susan and I like to hide under the bush.

Math is my favorite subject. Our first grade teacher is Ms. Hawking. Our test is on addition and subtraction. It is too easy for me. I finish the test long before anyone else. I look around the room. They are all still working. I wait for someone else to finish. I see at the bottom of the mimeographed page a series of letters and numbers. I look at my answers to the test for a second time. I notice my answers and the letters and numbers at the bottom of the page have some kind of connection, a relationship. They are the same length and repeat in the same way. Then it comes to me. They are the answers to the test—in secret code. I figure out the code while everyone else finishes the test. I take my test paper up to Ms. Hawking and tell her about my discovery. She grabs my test paper and hollers at me to get back to my seat. She collects all the tests and leaves the room. She returns in a few minutes with shorter papers. The bottom part of every page has been cut off. She hands back the papers to everyone but me. She calls me up to her desk and says that she'll have to talk to my parents about this. I have no idea what I did wrong.

I have a big black rubber spider. It looks all hairy. It's cool. My mom and dad gave it to me for Halloween. It's my favorite toy. I show it to all the kids at school. They all think it's cool too. I think it would be funny if I put it on Ms. Hawking's chair. She sees it on her chair and picks it up and puts it in her desk drawer. I'm too afraid to ask for it back. I don't want to get into trouble. Ms. Hawking doesn't say anything about the spider. I know I will never see my spider again.

My mom tells me to read something while we wait. It will help the time pass, she says. We are at the hospital, the part of the hospital for children. I am going to have an operation. The doctor is going to take my tonsils out of my throat and put little tubes in my ears. I pick up a book of children's Bible stories and read a story about a little boy who is in the hospital and is very sick and is afraid he will die. His friend visits him and tells him not to worry about dying. His friend says that God will protect him. The boy is very sick and still very afraid. He worries that God will forget about him. His friend tells him that just before going to sleep he should prop up his arm by his side, so that it looks like he's raising his hand. That way, says the friend, God will know that you want his help and He will take care of you. The next day the little boy dies. But he dies with his arm propped up so his friend isn't too sad since God took care of him. I finish reading the story and I remind myself to keep my arms down while I'm in the hospital. I do not want to die.

I think basketball is my favorite sport. But I'm good at most all of them. The first time our gym teacher, Ms. Duggins, had me do the shuttle-run she said I was close to the school record. So I tried again. And again. She had me do it three times in a row. Each time she said her stopwatch said that I was almost there. I got tired. I never broke the school record but I was close. For field day I represented our school against all the other elementary schools in the high jump and the long jump. I was also the last runner—which means the fastest—on the four-man relay race. I won three blue ribbons that day. But basketball is my favorite sport.

I am a little nervous during tryouts. I know that I'm one of the best players in the school, but I am nervous all the same. I want to do my very best. I have to make the sixth grade team. I miss a lot of shots but other than that I play okay. Half of the boys can barely dribble. Keith Buckley fell down twice during the layup drill, tripped up by his own feet. I usually make more of my shots than I do during tryouts. We are all out of breath. At the end of the tryout, the coach reads off his list. I start to worry when my name isn't in the first five. He keeps saying other boys' names. This can't be happening. And then he finishes. He thanks us all for coming. He says something about the ones who didn't make it. We should keep trying. I try not to cry. I just want to get out of the gym as fast as I can. My best friend Bird runs up to me and says that he heard the reason I didn't make the team was because the coach doesn't like lefties. He never picks lefties, he says. I don't care why I'm not on the team. I'm not on the team. I didn't make the team. I missed some shots. I wasn't picked for the team. It's the worst thing imaginable. Keith Buckley made the team. It's not fair. I cry all the way home. Basketball is my favorite sport.

Ψ

YOU WERE THE firstborn. The genesis of a new, better generation. The future. The grand promise. And not only were you the first child born into your family, but you were the first grandchild—on both sides. Our golden boy. We all doted on you. We spoiled you. Our prerogative after all. Your birth order conferred both entitlement and responsibility. Such is life. I never once saw you act entitled. But it was like you were aware of the responsibility from a very young age. You were serious. Even as a little boy you seemed old, grave.

Oh, but you were a sweet, sweet child. So kind. So thoughtful. Oh, and so, so smart. Too smart for your own good, perhaps, if there is such a thing. It was like you were born with an understanding of how the world works: an innate recognition of the principle of cause and effect, and an astute social awareness. It was disarming at times.

I remember holding you in my arms. You fit into the crook of my elbow. You couldn't have been more than six months-old at the time. I was talking to you. I don't recall how I started. I was just talking. So you could hear my voice. None of that goo-goo coo-coo talk either, it was regular talk. I was talking about the weather or the news, whatever. I was talking to you like a normal person, like an equal, like a little adult. You weren't smiling, but you paid attention. You listened. You didn't take your eyes off me. You stared at my moving lips. You met my eyes. Stone-faced and content. It was as if you were waiting for your turn to speak. For ten minutes you listened to me prattle without once turning your head away. I don't even remember you blinking. And then, out of the blue, you started crying. I rocked you and tried to get you to stop. You were inconsolable. A minute or two later your mother ran into the room and swept you into her arms. I told her that I didn't know what had happened. I sat on the couch and tried to figure out what I had done to upset you. Your mother said that you were tired or hungry or some such nonsense. I knew better. I had done something or said something that set you off. I replayed my words. What had I been talking about? The Russians, that's it. And I realized the reason you were crying. It was that I started to talk about the Russians and the Cuban missile standoff. And it worried you. My God, you cried over the geopolitical superpower situation. Now whether you saw something troubling in my face or picked up a tone of fear in my words, I'll never know. The key here is that you knew. You were six months-old and you knew something was amiss. I watched my words around you after that.

For years following that incident I thought I'd instilled a debilitating fear in you. That somehow I had broken you. Ridiculous, I know. But nevertheless that's what I thought. For years.

Why? Why did I think that way? Well, for one, we couldn't get you to go trick-or-treating. Try as we may, you would not go up to the door on Halloween. All the other neighborhood kids, dressed as witches and vampires, princesses and ghosts, laughed and screamed, running from house to house, but my grandson, my Superman, couldn't be coaxed off of the sidewalk. We pleaded. You were well aware that there was candy for the taking. You wouldn't even follow your younger sister. You watched Susan bound up the stairs while you waited, hiding between your parents. Susan always brought back an extra piece of candy for you. Even your little sister felt sorry for you. If memory serves you were ten years-old before you got off the sidewalk and uttered your first 'trick-or-treat.'

You were very athletic. You were good at any sport you tried. It all came so easily. I thought there was a chance you might become a professional tennis player. You were the best player in town. I loved watching you play tennis. You, I think, had your sights set on basketball. But, it turned out, baseball trumped them all.

Your childhood was spent between the lines, either of a playing field or the pages of a book. You were passionate about both, equally. You always seemed to be somewhere else.

Your schoolwork was exemplary, especially in math. You were nine and you were solving problems that your parents and I had difficulty understanding. You would sit in your room for hours performing abstruse calculations. You would proudly show us your work. Baffled, we nodded in approval. Your parents bought you these advanced mathematics books so you weren't bored by the simple work your classmates were expected to do. You loved it. You ate it up. It was like you couldn't get enough.

I remember the time your parents told me that you came home with a math test score of twenty-four out of twenty-five and you were crying that it wasn't perfect. They said that you cried all night. The next day when you showed me the test I told you that everyone makes mistakes. No one is perfect. It's our job to learn from our mistakes so we don't make them again. It's okay for ten year-olds to make mistakes, I said. That made you cry again. To this day I don't know if you cried because you realized that you weren't perfect or you cried because you felt you'd let us down or you cried because you disappointed yourself. It was one tiny mistake, one answer on one test, in the third grade.

Oh, and you were so sensitive. Such a sensitive child. You took on the weight of the world.

When my wife, your grandmother Nina, died I asked your parents if you would be an altar boy for the funeral. I thought it would be sweet. Nina would've approved. But I wasn't in my right mind. I was only thinking about myself. I didn't think to ask you first. I just assumed you would do it. A month later I saw the burn scars on your hand and asked your mother what had happened. She said it was nothing. But I could tell that there was more to the story so I pressed. After some badgering, she told me that you had injured your hand on the incense holder during the funeral. She said that you'd never handled a thurible before and didn't know what to do. The chains slipped when the priest handed it you and the only way you could secure it was with your bare hand. You told your mother that you didn't want to do anything to spoil the service. You held that searing brass censer in your blistering hand until the priest noticed and took it away. You didn't make a sound, not a whimper. And you never said a word. You are such a kind, thoughtful boy. But that was a stupid thing to do. You should have let it fall.

Do you remember when I took you to the circus? It was held in the city at the old amphitheater. The building's now long gone. Such a shame. Such a stately building. Every summer the circus would come there for a week or two. Months in advance colorful posters would announce its arrival. There was even a big parade, elephants leading the way. I took you there when you were twelve or so. Your sister came too. I couldn't take just one of you. That wouldn't have been fair.

In the center of the stadium were the three rings, the main event, but the ramps and the concourses were lined with food stalls, sideshows and carnival games. Your sister was frightened by the brazen calls of the barkers. She just wanted to see the animals and the clowns.

We took our seats and eventually the clowns came out, most of them exiting from tiny cars. Lions, tigers and elephants were tamed. The jugglers entered the ring and you muttered something about projectile motion. The horse riders whipped around the outer rings and you told me that their centripetal acceleration kept them from falling. When the trapeze artists took over the center ring you whispered to me about linear momentum and pendulum motion. The acrobats drew gasps from your sister and the rest of the audience. You told me about center of mass and conservation of angular momentum. You almost took the fun out of being at the circus, but I could see that you were enjoying yourself. We both learned that the proper name for tight rope walking is funambulism. The ringmaster drew out the word like an incantation. Your sister was mesmerized.

You wanted to try all the carnival games. Games of skill, they call them. I told you that they were rigged. You thought they could be beaten with a combination of athleticism and calculation. I kept trying to tell you that they were fixed. They are meant to appear easy. That doesn't mean it's impossible to win, I said, but it's very difficult. You have to be lucky. As an example I explained the dart toss. Looks easy, right? I asked. How hard can it be to hit one of those balloons with the dart? But take a good look. What do you see? Right, they're moving. They are attached at the end so the air makes them move a little which reduces your chances of a direct hit. The tricky part, though, is when you do make a direct hit. Look again. The balloons are underinflated. See? Combine that with extremely light darts with points duller than spoons and you've got a rigged game. Even if you hit one of the balloons dead-on from the perfect downward angle, the dart would probably bounce off. You did not seem convinced or impressed by my explanation.

We walked around and I bought you both some pink cotton candy. Your sister's legs started to get tired and it was time to go. On our way out we passed in front of the Tubs-O-Fun game, where the object is to land a couple of balls into a peach basket. You asked me if you could try. I told you that it was rigged like all the other games, but you wouldn't listen. The man behind the counter overheard us. He said, come on kid, it's easy, watch. And he tossed one of the balls into the basket and it stayed in. He threw the second ball to you and said, go ahead I'll give you a free

15

practice toss. You didn't even look at me. You flipped the ball toward the top of the basket. It hit the upper side and landed softly, safely. See how easy it is, said the carny. You looked at me like you had it all figured out. You begged to play. You told me you couldn't lose. You said that the angle of incidence equals the angle of refraction. I told you that the game was fixed, that the only reason your ball stayed in was because his first ball deadened the bouncy basket. It was a set-up. You pleaded. I gave you the money to play. The man behind the counter called you a winner before he even gave you the balls. Here's our next winner! Step on up! You took your time and eyed the shot. You threw it perfectly, but it bounced out. You were incredulous. The second toss bounced out too. I didn't want to say I told you so. You're my grandson after all. I just said that it's time to go. I thought you were going to cry. You were angry that you weren't right. You'd been duped. It broke my heart. I just wanted you to have some fun. That was all. You didn't speak the entire ride home. Susan slept soundly, probably dreaming of clowns.

Of course you were an all-star. And you were an all-star among all-stars. You were the starting pitcher. You pitched two scoreless innings before you were pulled to give another boy, another all-star, his turn on the mound. Once you were on the bench I didn't care much for the game. I watched you. You seemed angry. You cheered for your team when it was appropriate, but most of your time was spent kicking the dirt and talking to yourself. You weren't sulking. You were angry. And I didn't know why. Your team was winning. You had done well. Maybe something else was troubling you. After the game I asked you if there was a problem. I told you that I'd been watching you kick the dirt and talk to yourself. You can talk to me, I said. You said that you were disappointed in the way you had pitched. I said that you had been brilliant. You said that you hadn't. You said you had walked one batter and made six other mistakes on various pitches. You told me that you were replaying your 'errors' in your head. You couldn't let them happen again. You might not be so lucky the next time. I said that from my perspective, and probably everyone else's at the ballpark, you were impressive. One boy out of seven reached base—on a full count walk. And only first base at that. That's pretty darned good. Remember, you were pitching against other all-stars, I said. The best of the best. No slouches in that lineup. You said that it didn't matter and that I obviously didn't know what I was talking about. Just forget it, you said. I said sure and then I told you that I was sorry. I didn't know what else to say. You were so hard on yourself.

Toward the end, sports made you sad it seemed. Winning was treated as routine and losing was ruination. The better you became, the more emotional the competitions became. It was all or nothing. It was like watching that poor, doomed Janis Joplin sing. It was all grounded in pain. Maybe you got something out of it that I couldn't see. But I sure as heck saw the sadness and the hurt.

It got so bad that I had to stop going to watch you compete. I couldn't take it anymore. It was too much. I think almost ten years passed before I went to watch you pitch your last high school game.

I did my best to make you laugh. Maybe I didn't do the world's greatest job, but I tried. I tried to get you to lighten up and have some fun. I wanted you to see that life didn't have to be so serious all the time. That's what I tried to do. That's what grandfathers do. Well, yours anyway.

Ψ

YOU CAN HEAR the spin. It's a deep whistling whir, a whizzing, like the ball is slicing through the air molecules themselves. It's kind of cool. But to hear it it has to be quiet. And if it's really quiet, the kind of quiet you'd never experience in a game, the kind of quiet that exists when you are practicing, alone, you can actually hear the tonal differences between pitch types, between the different spins. It's fantastic. The music of the spin varies. A cutter is an octave above a slider and a change is a semitone deeper than a screwball. Each spin has its own signature sound, its own register. Every pitch plays its own music. It's beautiful. Well, I can hear the music. I've never asked anyone else if they've heard it. I keep it to myself.

Of course everyone can hear the pop when it hits the catcher's mitt. That's what people react to. That's the payoff. But it's the spin that gets you there.

Looking back I find it difficult to believe that I ever became a pitcher to begin with. I still remember the first pitch I ever threw. I was eight years-old. The coach told me to try out as a pitcher either because I wasn't any good at any of the other positions or because I was a rarity, a leftie. My first attempt at hitting the catcher's mitt almost sailed over the backstop. I tried too hard. I wanted to impress.

"Bosh, five more then hit the showers," yells Coach Penrose. "I want you fresh for tomorrow. A scout from U of I will be here."

"Okay, coach," I yell back. I gesture to the catcher with my glove that a curve is coming and I start my motion.

I am an athlete. I am a baseball pitcher. I throw a ball past batters who want to hit it. I'm good at pitching. It makes me popular. Plus, I love the physics. I like outsmarting people. And I'm in control. That's why I pitch. That's why I'm a pitcher.

Thornridge is our conference rival. We are tied atop the standings. They have a pretty good team and one really great pitcher. Man, he can bring it. Rumor has it that he's going to sign with the Yankees after the season. Luckily, he's not pitching today. So we should win. They're still a pretty good team though.

As I'm warming up in pre-game I watch the Thornridge players in their purple and gold uniforms step off the black and yellow bus. I purposely try to look each one of them in the eye to reinforce that they are in enemy territory and the next few hours will not be pleasant for them. I know. It seems silly, macho. Even juvenile. After all, their school is only ten minutes away, just on the other side of the expressway. We're neighbors. We live in the same town. We share the same McDonald's and see each other at the same Tastee-Freeze. We date each other's girls. Still, I find the stare-down helps me focus on the task at hand. It gets me pumped up, psyched. It sets the mood for us versus them. It's game time.

Our shortstop, my best friend Bird, whispers that there are two college scouts in the stands. I hit him on the shoulder with my mitt and say, "Maybe they're here to scout you." He laughs in staccato chirps. Bird is small and fast as lightening. He's got one of the greatest gloves I've ever seen. He's like a human vacuum cleaner. Knowing that he's there makes me a better pitcher. I never worry when a grounder heads his way. At the plate, however, it's another story. He slaps at fastballs like he's swatting flies and he whiffs at breaking pitches like his eyes are closed. His speed makes his batting average look better than it should. He's an above-average player and, most importantly, he loves the game. He'll probably end up playing D-3 ball somewhere.

I know the scouts are here to watch me. I used to get nervous about it. Now it's just bothersome, if anything. After so many I find it kind of funny that grown men have nothing better to do but watch some high-school kid throw a baseball. Absurdity settles the nerves. Coach told me about the guy from U of I, but I don't recognize the other guy. The scouts sit next to each other in the bleachers and I wonder whether they are friends or they're just pretending to be friends, just being professional. They are competitors after all.

Once the game starts I forget all about the scouts. Once I take the mound I forget about everything. It's like I'm on top of the world. I recognize that the mound itself is only ten inches higher than the plate. But in metaphorical terms it is much higher. It's more than just symbolic. I literally stand on higher ground than everyone else on the field. I am on top. I am in control. And it feels incredible. I get to call the shots. I determine how fast or slow the game moves. It all depends on me. It may be a petty power, but it is power, and for that half-inning that I'm on the mound, the world is mine.

The first few innings are uneventful. Their second baseman hit a lucky blooper over Hamilton at third. Our only base runner has been Bird who got hit by a pitch in the bottom of the second.

Things get interesting in the fourth inning. At least for us. The Thornridge pitcher, a lanky right-hander with a give-away delivery, walks one and falls behind our left fielder, Euler, but the pitcher gets lucky when Euler smacks into a fluky force at second. Next, my catcher, DeWitt, strikes out as usual. Bird follows with a squib to their pitcher who throws wildly allowing Bird to escape to second, Euler to third. The very next pitch is a cookie to our first baseman Deutsch and he doesn't miss it, sending it over the fence in left center. We lead three to nothing.

That's all I need to work around their hitters. It's so much easier pitching with the lead. It's much more fun too. I think one ball got hit hard all day and the guy pulled it foul. Before I realize what's happened, the final batter is at the plate. It's their center fielder and he's already struck out twice. This is the third time he's faced me but I can tell that he has no clue. I decide that this time I'll let him hit the ball. I won't let him reach base, but I'll at least let him say that he got a piece of me, once. Maybe I just want to prolong my stay on the mound. Maybe I don't want the game to end. I don't know. I call Bird over and tell him to be awake because I'm going to let the guy connect. Bird covers his mouth with his glove and tells me to take a look at the girl in the blue halter-top half-way up the stands. "How 'smokin' is she?" After Bird returns to his position I let the batter foul off two consecutive soft sliders before giving him a third in the same location taking just a little off of it. Predictably, he over-swings and taps the ball to the left side. Bird scoops up the weak grounder and throws a bullet to Deutsch at first. A cloud of rosin puffs out of the first-basemen's over-sized mitt with the pop. Game over. We shake hands with our vanquished opponents and mumble nice game, not really meaning it. We are alone in first place in the conference. Coach thinks we can win regionals.

In the dugout we shake hands, laugh and bro-hug talking about the win and the post-game party. Coach interrupts the celebration. The scouts, smiling broadly, flank him. One by one my teammates head off to the showers until I am left alone with the adults. Coach introduces the guy from U of I and says that the other guy is from Duke. The way coach talks I can tell that he's impressed by the visit. I thank them for coming out and they laud me with words I've heard before. The guy from Duke says that we'd have to work a little on strengthening but it shouldn't be a problem. I appreciate his candor. Then coach tells me to hit the showers and the scouts say that they'll be in touch.

We party after every game. Win or lose. We're jocks so we don't do drugs. We drink. And, boy, do we like drinking.

Bird picks me up in his noisy 1972 Ford Ltd. The muffler is missing and I hear him coming two blocks away. He looks even smaller in the gigantic brown car. He asks me for two dollars in gas money and says that we have to pick up Cruiser before heading over to Donna's house for the party. Bird hits up Cruiser for two bucks before he's half-way in the car.

"Two bucks! We're only going across town Bird. For two bucks I should at least get to sit in the front seat," he complains.

"Bosh called it first. And he didn't complain about

the money. Besides Podolski's bash is a kegger so you won't have to pay for drinks. It evens out, you cheap bastard."

"Evens out? Not for you. You come out way ahead," answers Cruiser.

"Not so much. My dad is boycotting Shell which means I have to drive out of town to fill up, so it costs me extra. Nobody's getting rich here, Cruiser."

"Why's he boycotting Shell?"

"Who cares?"

Donna's older brother—he graduated last year, the Class of '79—opens the door and before we can even acknowledge his presence he says, "Shit, I didn't know you guys were going to be here. I would've reserved another keg. Come on in Boshy. Guys."

The whistle from some Molly Hatchet song summons from the other side of the room where there's a circle of Thornton High School's finest athletes milling around a dented, dull silver keg of Budweiser. The television is on without sound and a few people watch the Cubs with Mike Krukow on the bump losing to the Reds. Someone hands us plastic cups and we join the circle.

Dan Wheeler, first string quarterback, pats me on the back and says, "Great stuff today."

"Thanks," I reply.

"Step back, everybody," announces Wheeler. "We need to fill this *pitcher* with beer," he says laughing.

Greg Rosen, starting point guard, grabs my cup and fills it with equal parts liquid and foam. "There you go, stud. Drink up, you've earned it."

I thank Greg and spy Bird and Cruiser thirstily waiting on an outer ring. I shrug my shoulders and move toward the television, beer in hand.

"Hey, Boshy, can I get you another one?" asks

Donna Podolski, our hostess.

"No, thanks Donna. Just got one. See," I say, showing her my cup of foam. "Thanks for having us over. Great bash."

"My pleasure. I'm happy you're here. Happy to have you. Have fun. Let's talk later, okay?"

"Yeah sure. I look forward to it," I say, taking an unsatisfying drink of foam while watching the buxom blond cheerleader bounce over to someone else.

"*En fuego*, my friend. Donna is fire," says Bird.

"Yeah, she is something," I answer as Krukow gives up another hit.

The tilted empty keg bobs in tepid water. Every few minutes someone tries to pump out a last cup. But it just sputters. It's dead. Bird and I sit on the couch. Whenever someone approaches the keg we yell, "It's dead!" But they try anyway. They can't help it. It's human nature. Worst of all is that it's too late to take up a collection for a second keg. The party is over. No booze, no party.

We head for the door. I try to talk Bird into driving me to Naugles Tex-Mex so I can get some late night food. He's tired and wants to go home.

Donna notices that we are leaving and comes running over. She thanks Bird before turning to me and whispering in my ear, "I wish you weren't leaving."

"Bird's my ride," I stammer, wishing I didn't have to leave.

"Another time, then," she says biting my earlobe.

I have been to Donna's house four times since her party. Her brother is back at college, her mom is always at work and her dad died of a heart attack when she was a little girl. The house is ours. We turn on the television, get comfortable on the couch and make-out until I can't take it anymore. We kiss so hard my mouth bleeds. I get the feeling that she wants more than kisses from me. Each make-out session is more passionate than the last. And each time she's wearing less clothing when she answers the door. The last time we didn't even turn on the television. She wants to have sex. I do not. I mean, I do want to have sex. There's nothing wrong with me or anything. But I don't want to have sex with her. Not now. Not yet. The truth is that I'm afraid to go any further. She's beautiful and sexy and, apparently, willing. But I'm not. I'm not ready yet. And the weird thing is that I don't know why I'm not. Maybe it's a lack of control issue? Yes, okay, I am afraid that she's more experienced and that I might not do it right. There's that. It's stupid. I should just do it and get it over with. I'm supposed to be some baseball stud, right? She is so hot. But I'd be doing it just to say I did it. And that's not right. It can't be. I rationalize that it's just not enough. Sometimes I hate being rational.

Head cheerleader Joy Hilbert tells me that Donna wants to break up. I tell Joy that I didn't even know we were going out. I play it cool and say that I thought we were just hanging out having fun. I tell her it wasn't serious. I tell Bird that I think Donna broke up with me because I wouldn't sleep with her. Bird calls me a pussy, which seems both ironically clever and cleverly ironic.

I like most of my classes at school. This separates me from most of the other jocks. My favorite class is physics with Mr. Minkowski. I like to know how things work. I lose myself in the equations. I daydream about the math. It may sound stupid but it's better than being on the mound sometimes.

"On the whole these papers are lousy," sighed Mr. Minkowski. "They are even—horror upon horror—worse than your previous assignments. Am I doing something wrong? I ask you. Are you all fundamentally stupid or do you just not give a damn?"

He tosses the papers back to my classmates. I don't get mine. I am about to raise my hand when I hear my name.

"The one exception, the single bright light in this dark cavern of ignorance is the work of Mr. Jerome Bosh," says Mr. Minkowski. "Mr. Bosh, I thank you for showing me that all hope is not lost. This is an excellent piece of work."

"Thanks," I say, receiving my paper.

"Mr. Bosh, since I seem to be failing miserably in my duties as an educator, perhaps you could assist me and enlighten your fellow students as to the proper construction and execution of this assignment. Please come up here and share your work with them."

"Sure, I guess," I reply heading to the front of the room.

"Um, my paper is on the physics of the baseball pitch."

I hear snickers in the back of the room and someone whispers 'typical meathead jock.'

I continue. "There are, as you probably know, too many variables, too many types of pitches, too many ways to throw a baseball to perform a comprehensive, detailed study. So, for this assignment, I simplified things and focused my analysis on the relative velocity and break of the common two-seam fastball based on various release points, also known as the arm slot angles. Now, for the purposes of this paper I assumed

27

a spin rate of . . . ." As I'm talking the class disappears and I turn my back to write on the board. I continue to speak but I'm not listening to the words. I'm lost in the diagrams and the symbols. I'm alone in a cloud of chalk dust. "So what this means is that for every two degrees the ball will . . . ." For a second I stop talking and look at what I've drawn and I catch a hint of something I missed or something I should've considered, but it disappears and I hear my voice again. "Then taking Bernoulli's principle into account we can see that . . . ." I hear groans behind me. I turn around. I should finish. "In conclusion, the optimum arm slot angle for the two-seam fastball depends on what you want it to do. And that's my paper, I guess."

"Thank you very much, Mr. Bosh. And that, class, is how you do physics."

"That's how you do baseball," someone laughs.

"Yes, and baseball. But it's the math that makes the paper, don't you see?" says Mr. Minkowski. "It's a simple idea. All brilliant ideas are simple. But it's the mathematics that shows us how beautiful and simple the world can be. And that's what we do in physics. That's what we try to do."

Our regional playoff game brings out more scouts. There are so many—they all look alike—that there might as well be none. Anyway, in such a big game there's no telling who they're here to watch. More importantly to me, my grandfather is in the stands. He hasn't seen me pitch in years. If we lose, this will be my final high school game. I guess he thought he'd better play it safe. He's never shown much interest in sports, though my mother told me that he once played golf with Al Capone. He must be here for me, I think.

Bird is psyched because there's some guy from

Elmhurst College here to see him. I want to tell him that Elmhurst is some middling college in another Chicago suburb and it'll be like he never left his hometown. But Bird wants to play ball somewhere. He's got to take what he can get. I've received offers from almost fifty major universities. I've narrowed it down to three. I haven't told anybody what the three are yet. Not even Bird.

"Make me look good out there, buddy," laughs Bird before we take the field.

"Ditto," I say.

After the *Star Spangled Banner* the team runs out onto the field. I walk. I take my time. This is my show now. My time.

The first inning is more about the umpire than the batters. As a pitcher the only thing you want from an umpire is consistency. I don't care if his strike zone is wide or high or low or narrow. I just want him to be consistent. I want to know that if I throw a certain pitch in a certain location I will get the same call. I can't be successful if I don't understand the umpire. So I spend the first inning testing him, a trial run. I pick at the corners, change speeds and alter my breaking balls. This leads to one hit and one walk but no real damage. On paper the inning may not look pretty, but once I know the umpire I can't be beat.

A quick three up three down for our side and I'm back on the bump for the second. This time I make short work of them. I strike out the side.

Bird walks in the bottom of the second but gets stranded after stealing second and third.

"The Elmhurst guy had to love that, right?" asks Bird as we take the field for the third inning.

"You're the wind, Bird. Look alive," I say.

The third inning is like the second. I strike out the

side. Walking back to the dugout I can hear the murmurs of approval. "Nobody can touch the guy." "Boshy's bringing it today." "I hear he's going to play for Stanford next year." I look up at my grandfather and he smiles and waves.

Their pitcher walks the first batter in the bottom of the third. The dreaded lead-off walk. A pitcher's worst sin. Two batters later Deutsch doubles him home. We lead one–zip.

I stroll out to the mound for the fourth inning. The buzz from the bleachers gets louder. I feed off the energy and throw a little too hard for a pitch or two. Then I settle down and, once again, strike out the side. There's a smattering of applause from the stands.

We get another run in the bottom of the fourth to lead by two.

Coach tells me to take it easy. "We've got 'em where we want 'em."

Bird is waiting for me on the mound. He hands me the pill. "Damn, Boshy, let them hit it once or twice, the rest of us would like to play too," he laughs, taking his position.

I strike out the first two batters in the top of the fifth. That's eleven in a row. I tell myself that it's bad luck to count. The next batter, their third baseman, looks at strike one—a cutter on the corner. I barely miss on the inside with a slider. My third pitch catches a little too much of the plate, but the guy pulls it foul. The count is one and two. He's mine, I think. I paint the outside corner with my next pitch. The umpire calls it a ball. He's been calling that a strike all game. Bad call. So I throw the exact same pitch again thinking there's no way the batter can lay off because the previous pitch was so close. The batter watches it hit the spot. The umpire calls it a ball. Another bad call, I think. The count is full. I've gone with the same pitch in the same spot two times in a row. The batter will be looking for something on the inner half, probably off-speed. But I have the lead. I can afford to gamble. This gives me the advantage. I decide to throw the same pitch yet again. I'm counting on the umpire to regain his consistency. Third time's the charm. I'm almost laughing to myself as I begin my wind-up. I release the pitch precisely where I want to. It flies true. The batter is fooled. His bat stays on his shoulder. The ball hits DeWitt's mitt with a loud pop. The umpire calls it a strike. Good call. Twelve in a row. More applause as I walk off the field.

Deutsch hits a homerun in our half of the fifth to put us up by three. Coach practically leaps out of the dugout to hug him. Everyone is smiling.

"Bosh, over here," says the coach after the third out. "We've got this one. I'm going to send Lorentz out there to finish. I want your arm nice and rested for the next game."

"Sure, coach, whatever you say," I say, though inside I'm disappointed.

Lorentz walks the first guy he faces but settles down after that. The second batter hits into a double play. The third guy, their catcher, hits a deep fly to center for the third out.

In our half of the inning Bird slaps a single between infielders. I clap for him. He looks toward the stands to see if the Elmhurst College coach saw his hit. The scout isn't there.

Three little outs and we move on in regionals. Lorentz fans the first guy. The second, however, reaches on an error and a third smacks a single. Coach goes out to the mound. He's nervous, I think. He comes back and says, "Boshy, one more base-runner and I'm pulling him."

The next batter walks. The bases are loaded. Coach sends in Reimann to pitch.

The stands are silent.

I know the first pitch from Reimann is going to be hittable. He will try too hard to get ahead in the count, I think. Sure enough, Reimann throws a cookie over the heart of the plate. The batter jumps on it and does not miss. We all turn to watch the ball sail over the leftfield fence. A grand slam. And, just like that, we are losing four to three.

Reimann somehow manages to calm himself and get the third out. All of us on the bench clap and chatter trying to psyche each other up. "Come on. We've got three outs to get two and win this thing." "We can do this." "This is why we worked for home field." "We can still win." "Never give up. "We can do this." "Come on now." "Let's do this."

But there are no heroics. No one even reaches base. The game ends. We lose. And it hurts.

All the joy is on their side of the field.

It's a tough loss. Brutal. I feel sorry for Reimann. It can happen to anyone. We all lost. Win as a team, lose as a team. I can't say that to Reimann though. It won't make him feel any better. Only time can do that. Then it dawns on me that I'll never throw another high school pitch. Our season is over. This part of my life is over, I tell myself. I pick up my glove and head for the showers. I see a group of scouts waiting by the gym entrance.

My grandfather stops me and says, "Good game, Jerry, I'm sorry your side lost."

Ψ

MY MOM MADE me be your friend. You know that, right? And I never even thanked her. Not once. Come to think of it, I never thanked my mom enough. That's on me, I guess.

Anyway, it was first grade and you had moved into the ranch house on the corner, the one without a garage or a fence, the Clifford's old house. My mom saw you standing in the backyard. She told me to go and make friends. Go on over there, Steven. He's the new kid in town; he's probably scared and lonely, she said. Dude, did she have it wrong.

I didn't get you at first. You were different. You were weird. You were polite and stuff. Even though you were new to the block you seemed already at home. Like it was no big deal whether you were here or there. I asked you if you wanted to play and you said if it was what I wanted. Then you introduced me to your parents. Weird. We were six, dude. What six year-old introduces another six year-old to his parents? You were strange, a real oddball.

At school it was more of the same. The weirdness continued. On your own planet. You talked to the teachers, man, like they were regular people. The teachers. And you knew the answers to all their questions, no matter what the subject. The rest of us thought you must've come from some superschool where they taught you better. Some of the kids made fun of you. They said you were an alien or a robot. You didn't care or you pretended not to care. I wanted to tell them to stop, but I didn't. Then one day at recess you left planet Bosh and joined in our game of tag. You were way faster than any of us. We played another game. You were better at that too. I threw you the basketball and we watched you sink a free throw. Like it was no big deal. A regulation free-throw from a six year-old! I couldn't even get close to the rim from that distance and I was good. I never saw anyone tease you again. Ever.

Best friends since the first grade. Obviously, dude, I got used to the weirdness. The better I got to know you, the less weird you seemed. Less weird, but more amazing. You were great at everything. If we weren't playing sports, you tried to talk to me about math. Math! You were a kid but you weren't. If that makes any sense. It was like you were a superhero. Everything came easy for you. And not once did you brag or act like you were better. You were just you. You were just Bosh. You were cool about it. I knew I was lucky to be there, to get to hang out with you. But do you want to know something? You want to know a secret? Sometimes I hated you for it. Dude, it wasn't your fault, but I felt like a sidekick, like number two. No, not like shit. Like I wasn't as good. It wasn't you. It was me. There were times I wanted to be you or more like you. I wanted to be better. I wanted to have your powers. I wanted to be cooler. I wanted to be the hero. Like that Halloween with Buckley.

34

First, you let Buckley tag along with us when we went trick-or-treating. No one liked the kid. No one liked him in grade school and no one liked him any better in high school. But you said it was okay for him to be with us. Buckley beamed. I wanted it to be just the two of us. Yeah, I know. Like I had a crush on you. Sure, a teen bromance. Sorry, dude, not my type. We were older and it was probably our last time trick-or-treating. We must have been thirteen or fourteen.

Buckley was a zombie. His mom had done his make-up. I was a vampire. My cape kept twisting in the wind. The plastic teeth hurt so I kept them in my pocket until we knocked on the door. Then I'd pop them in. You were dressed as Albert Einstein, with little glasses, crazy hair, a big, bushy mustache and a long, white lab coat. In three hours we hit half the doors in town. Our brown, double-bagged, shopping bags were loaded with loot. It got late and we headed home. When we were cutting through the field by the school some older kids came running after us. They were after our loot. We ran. You were gone like a shot. I might not be as fast as you, but I'm pretty fast. There was no way they were going to catch me. We ran for a bit till we were sure no one was chasing us. We were both out of breath. Then we went back for Buckley. He wasn't so lucky. He was on the ground crying. Make-up was running down his face. His bag of candy was gone. The older kids had taken it. You helped him up, told him to stop crying and gave him your bag. The whole bag. I felt sorry for him too, but who does that? Who gives it all away . . . to Buckley? Dude, it was probably his own fault he got caught anyway, probably tripped over his own feet.

I had the best seat in the house. Behind you. At short.

All those years watching you pitch and I never could figure out how you did it. You were more than all the pieces. I saw guys who threw harder, guys who had better stuff, but nobody pitched like you. You had it all. I would put myself in their place and even though I knew what pitch you were going to throw, in my imagination, I never got a single hit off you. It was like you were a magician. I don't know how you did it. They were always off balance. You were always ahead. And then all the attention you got. It was unreal. And you treated it like it was normal. No, you treated it like it didn't matter. All those people. Telling you this, promising you that. You treated it like it didn't matter. But it mattered. It mattered to them. And it mattered to the rest of us. You could've gone pro. You would've gone pro. That would've been cool. Dude, that would've been sweet. My best friend a pro ball player. Nice.

So you were better at sports, better at school and an all-around better person than me. Fine. That was okay. I was better with the ladies, wasn't I? I had a gift, didn't I? Okay, not a gift so much as a lack of fear maybe. I tried. I worked at it. You didn't have to. Chicks threw themselves at you and you didn't seem to notice. Again, you didn't seem to care. For a while I thought that maybe hot chicks were your Kryptonite. Maybe they weakened you, turned you into a mortal like the rest of us. But I was wrong. You were just playing it cool. You dabbled, didn't you? But you had your mind on other things. You couldn't be bothered by the smokin' hotties hanging on your every word. They bored you. Fine. Listen dude, I was happy to pick up the slack. You didn't care. You were above it all. Okay, I'll even admit you're better looking. So you've got that too. Happy? If I didn't know you I'd say that you were showing off.

You probably saved my life too. Do you know that? Do you remember?

I was on my front porch. I said let's go before you could ask why an ambulance was in my driveway. You knew enough to keep quiet. And you never pushed me to talk if I didn't want to. Dude, we walked for hours. I didn't say a word. We went back to my house and I told you to wait while I went into the garage. It was dark by then. Night. All the lights in the house were off. The ambulance was gone. No one was home. I came out with a bag in my hand and I told you to follow me. We ran to the field behind the elementary school and hid by the backstop. I showed you the gasoline bomb I had in the bag. I asked you to light it for me. I just wanted to watch it hit the ground and explode. I needed to see it. I needed to watch it burst and burn. You lit the rag fuse and, as I went to throw it, gasoline spilled out onto my shirt. I was on fire! You threw me down on the ground and rolled me over. That put out the fire. I didn't have a mark on me, not a single burn on my shirt. It was a miracle, I thought. Then I cried and told you how my mom had taken too many pills on purpose and was rushed to the hospital. I told you how she'd been sad for a long time. I never said thank you enough to her. You told me that it would be alright. And it was, eventually. You saved my life. You saved me from the fire, yeah. But, more than that, you saved me from myself. Dude, I was so mad that night. I couldn't see straight. I had no idea what to do. You talked me down. You told me that you were there for me. You told me what I needed to hear. You know, when I was with you it felt like I could do anything, like I could take on the world. Maybe that's what real friendship is.

That thing was like a boat, wasn't it? That big, bad, brown Ford Ltd. Remember how loud it was? Steering that thing was like sailing on the ocean. It was all over the place. And it was so big. I know. And I'm so small. I'll tell you what, though, I never felt bigger than when you were in the front seat next to me. I may have looked small, but I never felt bigger. Why would I want to flatter you? It's true. Some of my happiest times were the two of us in that car just driving around and talking. We'd cruise around looking for the action. I know, different times, right. Dude, there were no cell phones then, no text messaging, no apps to plan hook-ups, to set-up meeting places. We cruised in the LUK 112—the license plate, remember?—to the usual spots looking for anything fun: we drove past Spinner's Arcade, through the McDonald's parking lot, by the Tastee Freeze, past Pirani's Pizza, around the high school, next to the woods. Dude, I spent half of everything I had on gas money. We were so lame. But we would talk, wouldn't we? We would talk about everything. I remember talking about the future when you were trying to decide where to go to school. Yeah, it was before you'd decided on Princeton. You could've gone anywhere you wanted. I was a little jealous, I guess. And I was going on and on about playing ball somewhere, bragging about the few half-offers I'd gotten. Dude, I would've done anything to play pro, even if it was only in the minors. I just wanted to play ball for the rest of my life. I didn't care if I got paid. I didn't care if I was poor. You listened to me and then you told me life is long. You told me to make sure I went to the best school I could. You made me promise that I'd have a Plan B, in case the baseball thing didn't work out the way I wanted. Boy, am I glad I kept that promise. Life is long.

It was after Joy and I got engaged that she told me about what happened between you two. Years after the fact, in fact. I thought I knew everything about you . . . and her. I still can't believe I married the head cheerleader. Dude, and she's still fire. How cool is that? I know. I don't even remember where we were at the time and I don't know how it came up, but I had said something about you and she blurts out the whole story. I can't believe you never told me. You still don't know? It was our high school graduation party. Yeah, the one Deutsch threw at the woods. His dad's bar donated the beverages. The drinks flowed. Dude, I was so drunk. We all were. I remember Rosen puking next to a tree and then lining up for another beer. Mostly it was all those watermelon shots. Man, we must've gone through two coolers of that stuff. The girls drank it like pop. Sweet and sticky. You couldn't taste the booze in it. And I think we went through two or three kegs. The weather was perfect. We played Frisbee and talked sports. We ate dogs and burgers and gallons of potato salad. I tried to hit on Donna but she wouldn't bite. It was one of the last times we'd all be together. And we partied like we knew it. There was garbage everywhere. Some of the girls tried to clean up but the trash cans couldn't hold it all. People started leaving after the sun went down but some of us stayed. We were all so drunk talking about the past and the future. It was the kind of night you wanted to last forever. But nothing lasts forever, does it? We began to pair off. Girls and guys. Dude, even me and you were a pair. We laughed at how drunk everyone else was. We were just as drunk though. You went into the woods to take a piss. Your fifth, you said. I turned to Deutsch and told him that I didn't think I could take another sip of beer. I was full. He called me a pussy and started singing Bowie. *Cha-cha-cha-changes!* And that's when it happened. Do you remember? Well, Joy does. She said she'll never forget it. You walked into the woods to piss and saw her and Wheeler going at it. Only Joy wasn't into it. She was crying and screaming but Wheeler—that asshole!—wouldn't take no for an answer. His was tearing at her clothes. He had her pinned to the ground. She was trying to fight him off. He was going to rape her, wasn't he? That's what Joy thought. And then you stepped in and grabbed Wheeler by the neck and flipped him over like a rag doll. Joy said you knelt down on him, grabbed him by the throat and roared at him. She said you told him that if you ever saw him do anything like that again to anyone, you'd kill him. The dude was way bigger than you and you were drunk. But you weren't scared. No, not Boshy. You took Joy by the hand and led her out of the woods. Not only that but you made sure that she got home okay. I had no idea why we were walking her home. I thought you had a thing for her or something. And you never said a word. Weird how life turns out, isn't it? You saved my wife. But you didn't know she'd be my wife. And I didn't know you'd saved her for me. My best friend and my wife. Who knew? Well, thanks. I know, dude. Just let me thank you for it, okay?

Ψ

"A LITTLE BIRDIE told me that you were once an athlete," she says running her index finger down my sweating chest.

"That was somebody else," I reply coyly.

"You've still got the body of one."

"Seen many naked athletes, have we?"

"My fair share," she says. We both laugh. I roll her on top of me and we make love again.

Her name is Elaine Mae Turing. And she's at Princeton working on her MA in English. *James Joyce: Accidental Misogynist* is her latest project. We met six weeks ago at a graduate student get-together on campus. I usually don't go in for such events, but I'd been sequestered for months writing my dissertation. It was time to come up for air. It was time to interact with other human beings. We've been interacting ever since.

My paper, treatise really, is tentatively entitled, *Worlds of Difference: Measuring Wavefunction Decoherence.* The idea developed from a thought I had when I was an undergrad reading about the life of Portuguese poet Fernando Pessoa. His *Book of Disquiet* is a classic. Well,

41

for artistic and aesthetic reasons he created all these very different writers with different lives and different styles. He called them heteronyms. The suggestion that we might have all these other lives, different but similar, made me wonder about what that would look like in physical terms. This, in turn, led me to the world of quantum mechanics and Everett's wavefunction decoherence. Although I've been working on the paper for the past eighteen months, it is the culmination, the climax, the grand fulfillment of nine years' worth of insightful, thoughtful philosophy, physics and, of course, mathematics. It's ground-breaking. It's almost finished. And it's brilliant.

Elaine buttons her shirt and scans the bedroom for her shoes. They are behind the door. She slips them on and reaches for the door handle.

"I suppose you are going back into dissertation hibernation," she says.

"I really need to be done with this," I say missing her before she's even left. "Don't take it personally. Once it's finished, I'm all yours. You'll be sick of me you'll see me so often."

"Ah, the irresistible promise of illness. Count me in," she laughs.

"I've just got to get Susskind on board with my conclusions and I'm done. You understand, don't you?"

"I understand that I like you more than I should. Fret not, Jerome, I shall be here when you awaken from your hibernation."

We kiss and I watch her hop down the porch steps and skip toward the street. I keep watching in the hope that she will turn around. She does. I smile. She smiles back.

In my mind the dissertation is finished. The paper is written. It is complete. The calculations, the graphs, the acknowledgments, the references are all perfect. And I am currently on a seventh revision of the abstract. I should be done. I feel like I should be done. My advisor, Dr. Susskind, however stands in my way. He keeps delaying the process, continually asking for what I consider arbitrary edits and changes. I feel he is intentionally sabotaging my work. I keep this feeling to myself. He should be my champion, but he has become my nemesis. I stay the course. Science is on my side. Truth is on my side. I will be victorious.

My paper resurrects a controversial theory—the Many Worlds interpretation. Ergo, I understand Susskind's trepidation. I fully appreciate his reticence. Careers have been destroyed by less. My career, however, will be celebrated one day. Of this I am certain. Susskind's can only be tarnished by the sensation my paper will undoubtedly generate, for I am breathing life into an idea most physicists want dead. I need to resuscitate the theory so I can explain how it is testable. And once it's tested, and if I'm right, the ramifications will be revolutionary.

The Many Worlds interpretation (MWI) is one of several competing arguments seeking to make sense of quantum mechanics. In short, MWI posits that every possible quantum outcome is realized. This takes care of the EPR paradox and Schrödinger's cat. It is neat, logical and elegant. Thus, in nearing an infinite number of universes, everything that could possibly have happened in our past, but didn't, occurred in the past of some other universe or universes. Done and done. Hugh Everett III formulated the idea right here at Princeton in 1957. Susskind was even a classmate of Everett's, a fact lost neither on me nor my advisor.

Everett's interpretation was not embraced. His mentor called the idea mad. Everett visited Niels Bohr and the Copenhagen crew and was treated like an insane heretic. They laughed at him. Well, Everett will have the last laugh. My paper proposes the way to test MWI. My position is that a combination of reversible nanotechnology and artificial intelligence is enough to test his theory. And I've discovered the key to marrying the two technologies. The logic is incontestable. Now, even with my idea, we are not yet there. But given Moore's Law and the AI climate, we will be able to perform my experiment in the near future—in my lifetime. See, all you have to do, once you have the machine, is to measure the spin of an electron along the z axis and record whether it's up or down. Next, you measure the spin along the x axis and record if it's left or right. The machine then reverses the entire x axis measurement. Finally, our amazing machine takes a spin measurement along the z axis and records it. Now according to the Copenhagen interpretation the first and last measurements only have a fifty percent probability of agreeing. But according to MWI, the first and the last measurement will always agree—one hundred percent of the time— because there is no collapse of the wavefunction. This result is only explainable with MWI. Talk about an original contribution to human knowledge! One of the great mysteries of physics will thus be answered. If the first and last measurements always agree, the wavefunction does not collapse. It's that simple. Decoherence replaces collapse. The implications are endless, no pun intended.

"For the nth time, Jerome, I do not have an issue with your work. The work itself is solid. My problem is your conclusion and your perspective on further progress in the field. You are young and ambitious, but temper your enthusiasm, young man. Manage your expectations. Set your sights with a little more, shall we say, acuity. Show a modicum of modesty. That's all I'm suggesting," says Dr. Susskind from the comfort of his leather office chair.

"I don't believe that I am being unrealistic in my conclusions," I say.

The office is small and cluttered. There are two framed photos on opposite walls. The first is Susskind as a graduate student posing with Einstein. The second is Susskind shaking hands with President George Herbert Walker Bush. I will not be intimidated.

"I'm not talking about realism here. I am talking about politics. We both know that your work will, to put it mildly, unnerve our community. You will create instant enemies. I'm just asking you to acknowledge this and tread a little more lightly. There will be time to trumpet in the future."

"I don't want to trumpet. I hope to inspire," I say sounding immodest even to myself.

"You are launching a career, not a blitzkrieg," he says.

We go round and round, again.

"With all due respect, I am starting to feel that you are looking for ways to kill my work," I say.

"Nonsense. I am your advisor."

"Is it about Everett?"

"Everett? Why would it be about Everett?" he asks.

"You knew him," I say.

He takes a moment before answering. I realize I've gone too far. I realize that I'm wrong.

"Yes, I knew Everett. He was smart. It was the

1950s at Princeton. Einstein was here for God's sake," he says pointing to the old photograph. "Look, Everett was smart. But we were all smart back then. He was no different than anyone else here."

"I know that, of course. I simply thought that having a history might . . . I didn't mean you were jealous." Jealous. Why did I say that? Wrong word. Tendentious. I should have said tendentious.

"He was brash. I'll tell you that. You will likely be happy to hear that you two share that unenviable trait."

"I don't think—"

"You know what happened to your Everett, don't you?" he asks interrupting me. "He was so sure of himself, so convinced that he was right, that he went to Copenhagen to see Niels Bohr personally. Niels Bohr! Everett thought he could convince the great Bohr that he was wrong about quantum mechanics and that he, Hugh Everett *the third*, had the answer. They had no idea what he was talking about. Bohr thought he was an idiot. His colleagues said he had no grasp of quantum mechanics. They thought your genius Everett was a clown."

"Yes, but—"

"It made him leave the field. He gave up physics. Went into business, commerce. He ended up getting fat, killing himself with drink and cigarettes. He died an unhappy nobody at the age of fifty-one. That was your Everett. Yes, he was smart. We were all smart," says Susskind turning away. "It was only a theory."

"I didn't mean . . . I think my paper is ready that's all. I have worked hard and I think my work is good," I say quietly.

He turns away from the window and looks me straight in the eye.

"Jerome, it isn't good work. It is brilliant. I am

46

honored to have helped in my small way. And for that reason I do not want it compromised by bombast or by what I am sure others will perceive as unnecessarily provocative conclusions. I am your advisor. I am advising."

"Thank you. I know. And I could not have done this without your mentoring, without your patience and assistance. It's just that I feel that for the past six months we've been at loggerheads and that I've been engaged in thesis defense rather than dissertation completion."

"Well then, you will be wonderfully prepared when the time for defense arrives, won't you?"

"Yes, I will."

"As far as I'm concerned, if you can rein in your enthusiasm in the conclusion a bit and show a tad more restraint in the further investigation section, the paper is publishable."

"I can do that," I say.

"Congratulations."

"Congratulations," says Elaine holding a bottle of champagne in her left hand.

She walks in, kicks off her shoes and heads straight for my kitchen. She is wearing black tights that end at the top of her calves and a gray school sweatshirt that is two sizes too big. The sweatshirt hangs suggestively off one shoulder. Her blonde hair pulled into a ponytail prances behind.

"So, how does it feel?" she asks.

"Good. No, great. To be honest it feels like a huge weight has been lifted off my back," I say. "I feel liberated. There were times I didn't think I'd ever finish."

She hands me the bottle to open and reaches

above the sink for glasses. The raised sweatshirt bares her taut curves.

"This looks like good stuff," I say not looking at the label.

"It's not every day my boyfriend submits his Ph.D. dissertation, is it?"

We drink the bubbly sitting on the couch. The B-52s tells us to 'roam if we want to' in the background. Her selection. She congratulates me again.

"I'm so proud of you. Congratulations. I know it was difficult. Here's to you," she says.

"Thanks. And I'm sorry the past six months have been so crazy. I would have much preferred spending time with you. The thought of being with you kept me going, you know."

"That's sweet," she says putting her hand on my leg.

"It's the truth," I reply lost in her eyes.

"Tell me," she says breaking the spell, "what is this awful paper about anyway? I know it has to do with quantum physics, but, specifically, what did you do? What's so important? Feel free to give me the truncated version. The big picture, not the nuts and bolts. When drinking I tend to get lost in the details."

"Okay, well, in a big nutshell, quantum mechanics has a wavefunction issue. Already too technical. Okay, take two. Quantum mechanics is wonderful. We know a lot about it and it helps us make incredibly accurate predictions about the physical world. It works. But there is a problem. It is based on probabilities and these probabilities when measured become reality, i.e., they cease being probable and become actual. Physicists call this measured reality a wavefunction collapse. And no one has really come up with a good reason *why* the wavefunction collapses."

"But you did?" she asks.

"No. Not really. There's a theory from the 1950s called the Many Worlds interpretation. And it claims that the wavefunction doesn't collapse at all. Rather, it undergoes decoherence, which means instead of collapsing it splits off into branches, like a tree."

"And each *branch* then is a new, separate world. That's how you get *many* worlds," she says.

"Precisely. There is no collapse and that means that every probability is realized. Everything that is possible happens, but in a different world. Everything plays out somewhere. In some worlds I do not tear my ulnar collateral ligament and I become a professional baseball player instead of a physicist. In another world I win the Nobel Prize. In yet another world we do not meet. All the possibilities of the wavefunction occur."

"Fascinating. I'm still with you and, for the record, I'm glad we met in this world anyway. Okay, so where does your work fit into all of this?"

"The Many Worlds interpretation has its own problems, one of which is that it can't be tested. As you can imagine this is kind of a drawback in science."

"Yeah, that might be an issue," she laughs.

"In my paper I propose a way to test the theory, and, more specifically, how to design a machine to test the theory."

"That's amazing," she says taking a sip from her glass. "So when does this machine get built? And can you name it after me?"

"Oh God, it's not that easy. It'll be years, decades, before someone will be able . . . I mean I may not live to see the day. It'll be a long time. But I've kind of started the journey with my paper. I've provided a roadmap."

"Oh, how disappointing. So it probably won't be

named after me. That is a shame. Okay, if someday someone does create your machine and tests the theory and the theory is true, what does that mean?"

"It will mean everything," I say. "We will have solved one of nature's great mysteries. It will open doors we didn't even know existed. It will change the way we look at the world and ourselves. It suggests the possibility of immortality for instance."

"Pretty weighty implications there, moral and otherwise. I don't know if people are ready for immortality yet."

"I leave that part to the philosophers and the writers. I'm just the math jockey here."

"What now?" she asks.

"Huh?"

"What now?" she repeats. "What's next?"

"Wow. I hadn't thought that far ahead to tell the truth. I guess I should find somebody who'll help me build the thing. And pay me for the pleasure, of course."

"Of course," she says kissing me on the neck.

"I'm going to have to find a job, aren't I?"

"Come on, the bottle's empty. Let's take the celebration to the bedroom."

She reaches for my hand.

"I love being with you," I say.

"I love you too," she replies.

"I said—"

"I know what you said, Jerome," she interrupts with a seductive laugh. "Come on."

I fiddle with the placard that reads: Jerome Owen Bosh, Princeton University. My name's acronym tells me to get a job. Or perhaps it gives me the patience of Job. I sit behind a long table next to Susskind who has his own placard with Dr. in front of his name. Two other physicists, both doctors too, are at the table as well. The first is Robert Hughston, an English physicist who's done some interesting work on the concept of time. The second is Scott Weinberg from Cal Tech. His research involves the hunt for extra dimensions. The panel is sponsored by the physics department, part of a general outreach program. The discussion is titled: *Beyond Experience: Science Outside the Senses.* Susskind is the moderator. The auditorium is full. Elaine waves to me from the fifth row. I nod. She is flanked by her parents who are visiting from Wisconsin. I assume that they are already bored. Susskind convinced me to be on the panel. He thought it would help promote my paper. After I accepted, I pointed out to Elaine that the discussion's acronym reads, 'BESOTS.' We plan on going out for a drink after it's over. Susskind introduces us and we each give a brief overview of our work for the audience of laypeople. We try not to make it too technical, but it's difficult to be general, thorough and clear without some jargon. As the hometown boy I get the loudest applause. Before long it's time for the questions, the interactive part of the presentation. We get the comments typical from those without a foundation in physics or mathematics.

Hughston spends a full five minutes patiently reiterating his contention to a confused questioner.

"Therefore, as you can see, time does not in fact exist," he concludes for the fifth time.

"But you can't really be saying that time doesn't exist," urges the confused man in the audience.

"That is precisely what I have been and am saying," he says.

"Well that's just crazy," says the guy sitting down.

"I'm sorry you feel that way," says Hughston.

"You may be interested to know that I'm currently at work trying to show that matter does not exist either."

"Now that's crazy," I interject, trying to be funny. No one but Hughston laughs.

Susskind attempts to move things along, but we are mired in ignorant disbelief. Almost every question is asinine.

"If we can't see the extra dimensions then who cares?" a young lady asks Weinberg.

"The existence of these extra dimensions gives us a better framework for understanding nature," he says.

"Not my nature," she shoots back. This gets more laughs than my crazy jibe.

A middle-aged man forces me to defend the idea of quantum immortality.

"You'll be dead to everyone, but yourself. Is that the idea?" he scoffs into the microphone.

"Generally, that's the idea, yes" I answer.

"Balderdash."

"Imagine this," I say. "Imagine that I have a gun. But the gun I have is no ordinary gun. It is a lethal quantum gun. And that means that the gun is controlled by a single particle and this single particle moves up and down in such a way that the gun has a fifty percent chance of firing when I pull the trigger. Up it fires, down it doesn't. And when it fires you are dead. Okay? With me so far? Good. Now if I point the gun at you and pull the trigger it has a fifty percent chance of not killing you. After a second shot you would have a twenty-five percent chance of not being killed. After ten shots the chance of you surviving drops to just one-tenth of one percent. This is just math, right? Well, in the Many Worlds interpretation, the particle in our gun doesn't have to choose between up and down. Both exist all the time. Up and down. So no matter how many times I shoot you, no matter how many times we all see you die, there will be instances— however few—when the gun doesn't fire and you don't die. And that's *your* reality. That makes you immortal. The downside is that you would never be able to get anyone to believe you. You may not even believe it yourself. Nevertheless, there it is."

"Prove it," says the man before sitting down.

"That's what I'm trying to do," I reply. "Or disprove it, really. That's what we are all trying to do."

Susskind wraps things up with customary words of thanks to audience and panel alike. I vow never to participate in a lay panel again. I walk backstage and hunt for Elaine and her parents.

My paper proves popular. I am relieved and vindicated. Susskind appears thrilled by the reception. The string theorists embrace me. I receive teaching offers from most of the major research institutions. I also get offers from abroad. I am wooed. I am invited to dozens of universities and institutes. I am offered handsome honoraria for my appearances. The experience reminds me of my baseball days. Coaches and scouts have become professors and deans. Their smiles are the same. I create a shortlist and discuss it with Elaine. I want her thoughts.

"What about MIT?" I ask.

"I'm not a big fan of Boston," she says. "Too many students. It creates a bifurcation. There's an 'us versus them' mentality. It's like two different cities."

"Well then, that takes care of Harvard too," I say.

"Wait, wait, wait," she starts. "That's just my opinion. This is about you and where you'll be the happiest. You have to think of the best fit for you and your work."

"Stanford?" I suggest.

"California? Really. Need I say anything more," she responds laughing.

"The Max Planck Institute?"

"In Germany? Do you speak German?

"I could learn," I state.

"What about here? Certainly they've made an offer. Or are you too good for New Jersey now that you're such a hotshot?" she asks.

"I love it here. You, of all people, know that. But I've been here for a decade. And that's long enough. If I really want to explore my ideas I have to get away from here and away from Susskind. It's time for me to leave," I explain.

She goes quiet. I wait a pregnant minute before speaking.

"What about the University of Wisconsin?" I propose.

"In Madison? My hometown? Have you lost your mind? No offense, but it doesn't exactly have the cachet, the elite ring, of the others, does it?"

"Not yet, no. They've offered me something no other school has though. They will give me my own department. I'll be in charge. They want to bring world class research physics to their school. They want me to be part of creating a new tradition. And I am a good Midwestern boy at heart, you know. The thought possesses a certain appeal, don't you think?" I ask hopefully.

"A little," she says softly. "It depends on what you want."

My parents and my sister fly in for the commencement ceremony. I give them roles to play in my planned production. They are happy for me.

Elaine is the first to greet me after the ceremony. She embraces me as if she'll never let go.

"I am so proud of you," she says with a kiss.

Out of the corner of my eye I spy my family approaching. I wink. I allow them to get a bit closer before speaking.

"Mom, dad, Susan!" I shout.

Elaine turns to greet my family. I disrobe—quite literally—revealing a period costume a friend liberated from the theater department. I am dressed as an early nineteenth century landed gentlemen—Mr. Knightly to be precise. Elaine turns around. With great flourish I drop to one knee and take her hand in mine.

"If I loved you less, I might be able to talk about it more. But you know what I am. You hear nothing but truth from me," I recite.

"Austen," she whispers. "I adore Austen."

"The truth, Elaine Mae Turing, is that I cannot live without you. The truth is that I love you more each and every day. The truth is that I want to spend the rest of my life with you? Elaine, will you please be my wife?"

There are tears in my eyes when I finish. I can't see her clearly, but I can hear her perfectly.

"Yes. Of course I will, you marvelous man. I love you so much. Yes. Yes, I will marry you."

I rise to kiss her. We hold each other tightly for what seems an eternity before the world intrudes.

She cries and wipes her eyes. My dad shakes my hand in congratulations. My sister hugs and kisses Elaine before stepping aside so my mother can embrace her daughter-in-law to be. They shed tears of joy, together.

Ψ

HAVE YOU AN inkling of the myriad students to have passed through these hallowed doors? Brilliant young minds, eager to please, begging to learn. I hesitate—no I refuse—to attempt the calculation. They are best left to the past. You see, in the final, and might I add, lamentable analysis, the preponderance of the students were but numbers. You, however, you Jerome, were anything but a number.

Our academic liaison was not without its twists and turns, though, was it? I recollect our first meaningful interaction as if it were yesterday. You still possessed the robust odor of the baseball diamond on your person. It was a graduate seminar on the philosophy of physics. As I was wont to do at the time, unannounced I arrived in your classroom to lend an air of gravitas and intellectual authority to the discussion. Your professor—it was that dolt Jordan—introduced me, appropriately, if maladroitly, as the distinguished and respected head of the department, Dr. Milton Susskind. Most of you were too frightened to speak in my presence. Those few who mustered the ability, both the brash and the brave, were indulging in the usual, pedestrian graduate student blather. You know, posing jejune theoretics like, should the goal of science be that which is true or that which is useful? Or, how do the classical and quantum views of nature impact the way we see the world philosophically? The sterile discourse devolved into a rather callow debate on determinism versus non-determinism. With well-rehearsed solemnity I cleared my throat and entered the fray. The sound of my voice silenced the heartiest among you. I thought I had quashed the conversation. You, however, found the mettle. You were the only one to rise to the challenge. The class cringed. We argued, for lack of a better word. We replayed the Einstein-Bohr debates a bit, didn't we? I was Bohr and you, of course, were Einstein. You were young and bumptious, a determinist certain that there were absolute answers out there ripe for the picking. You were the alpha dog among the students and it was my responsibility to evince that I was the alpha dog of the physics department, if not the entire university. It was my role, my small part to play.

"Anyone who is not shocked by quantum mechanics has not fully understood it, said Bohr. Can you say that you fully understand QM?" I asked.

"No, sir, I cannot, but neither did Bohr," you answered. "After all, Bohr was reluctant to accept the concept of the photon, wasn't he?"

"Quite right. Initially. This does not, however, exclude him from the equation. The fact that he altered his opinion in the face of additional experimental evidence shows that he was anything but dogmatic. A mind with such plasticity can see around corners. His Copenhagen interpretation has stood the test of time, my young man."

"Probability without causality? From Bohr to Born. Everyone is so easily seduced by the probability density function. Einstein despised such nonsense," you said. "Bayesian probabilities at best."

"Probabilities, sir, that have been uncannily accurate for more than half a century," I said.

"Cast a large enough net and you're bound to catch fish," you replied.

I said, "It seems to me and to most others in our profession that one must give up either locality or determinism. It has been my experience that most choose locality."

"What about Many Worlds? It is local, realist and deterministic," you said.

I had not heard anyone speak seriously of the Many Worlds interpretation in years. I thought it had died a footnote's death. I was intrigued if nothing else. It brought back youthful memories.

"Such untestable meta-theories get us nowhere. The wavefunction collapses," I stated drily.

You then made a blunder. A common schoolboy error. And that was when I had you. Always know your sources, young man. And you thought you were being clever.

"The definition of insanity is doing the same thing over and over expecting different results, said Einstein."

"The definition may not be without merit and wit, young man," said I. "But it is not Einstein. You are making an erroneous attribution. Those words, if you must know, come from a Narcotics Anonymous pamphlet first published in 1983. And, as most of us are aware, Professor Einstein died in 1955. You are regurgitating a common canard. Always be certain of your sources, young man."

I'll admit repeating the phrase 'young man' was a bit pitiless.

You paused to gather yourself. But the brief battle, our first skirmish, had ended.

"One's choice of interpretation, it seems to me, is a matter of personal philosophical prejudice, not objective certitude," I said.

"But if the Hilbert space is precisely defined," you said.

"Nonsense," I said. "Bohr was right, Einstein was wrong. There is no way of exactly determining the outcome."

And then I rose from my chair. Jordan, relieved, obsequiously thanked me for joining the discussion. Your face was a shade of red. I nodded and left as if I had more important matters to consider.

What I presumed at the time to have been an offhand, if arcane, reference was in fact your religion. You became the talk of the department. Jerome Owen Bosh is resurrecting Everett and Many Worlds. You were pertinacious. You and MWI. You were like a dog with a bone. I attempted to lure you away with the meaty promises of string theory and supersymmetry. You were monomaniacal. You were so cocksure, so certain you were right, so committed. It was impressive. But it was also troubling. It bordered on the obsessive. That kind of faith can be destructive. I had seen it before. I vowed that I would not let you destroy yourself and your career over MWI. You, however, had taken an antithetical vow.

I am certain you were not aware that I broke protocol to be your doctoral advisor. I could see there was no turning you away from your mission. Perhaps I could make the path less dangerous. I tried.

And then—eureka!—you worked it out. You

found a way, by God. You managed to pierce the invisible.

I was in my office. You were not announced. You did not, as custom dictates, knock upon the door. You just burst through as if in a fever. You were in mid-sentence waving coiled sheets of paper, like a thick magic wand, in your hand. You threw the sheets onto my desk. Strokes and slashes on grid paper. I didn't say a word. It wouldn't have mattered if I had. You would not have heard. You were loud but clear. You commandeered my blackboard and outlined the solution. Your broad grin barely fit on your face. And then you collapsed in a chair. And you waited.

Ever since that day I have been trying to find a flaw in your discovery. To date your breakthrough has proven inviolate.

I was then, and will forever remain, wonderstruck by your innovation. It was, and always will be, formidable, monumental work. I trust my admiration is beyond doubt.

The dissertation, your paper, was another affair entirely. We fought. You must understand that your work was never at issue. It was solid, ingenious and original. No, it was not about the work. It was about the way you wanted it presented. It was about your message. Your early drafts were messianic. You unabashedly proclaimed yourself the herald of a new physics. You were too declamatory, too inspirited. I sought to temper that enthusiasm. You had to be more professional if you cared a whit about the paper's success or your own. Being a young man, you did not see it that way. You wanted to declare that a new age of physics was upon us. I explained that a dissertation was not for pontificating. I urged patience and restraint. You threatened to quit. You said that you'd go elsewhere. Where you were appreciated, you said. More than once you declared that you'd had enough. There were times I, too, wanted to surrender. We persevered, however. We survived. It was a landmark paper. I was both proud and happy, like a father must feel upon the birth of his first child.

You had to leave. Your future, your destiny was elsewhere. I would not have respected you if you'd stayed. There were too many big fish in this pond. You needed to be on your own. You needed a pond of your own. You would have said that you needed an ocean. Behind the scenes I called in a favor or two. You could have gone anywhere you desired. I was somewhat surprised that you chose the University of Wisconsin. At that point, however, I had yet to meet Elaine. Even as a young man, you apprehended that there is more to life than work. After you told me your decision I telephoned my counterpart at Madison and offered my support and assistance in whatever they needed to ensure your professional success. At the time my name on a grant application carried great weight. I wanted you to succeed. I wanted you to be happy.

Our relationship, such as it was, had orbited around work. We had discussed physics and mathematics to the exclusion of all else. It was forever about the mathematics, about an intractable problem or a promising solution. We had never taken the time to be social. Despite this history, I could not let you leave without saying good-bye. I could not let you leave without thanking you.

By the way, the restaurant is still there. Addis Ababa. I had never tasted Ethiopian cuisine until that night. Now, once in a while, I will stop in, alone, for a

61

quick meal and remember that farewell dinner. Elaine was so charming. She ordered for us all. It was the first time we'd really spoken. I hadn't known she was a scholar of literature. She was so kind and caring. She could see I was at a loss without utensils. She explained the East African customs, the importance of family and sharing and how to eat using the bread, the *injera*, as the lone utensil. She even demonstrated and broke off my first piece for me, gathering up some spicy chicken, *doro wat*, into a bite-sized portion. She would have put it in my mouth had I asked. She was terribly considerate. It was as if she didn't want me to sully my hands with it all. I could see what attracted you to her. She was vivacious and witty, smart and sweet. She radiated life. This was something we cloistered scientists are not used to. I will admit I enjoyed her attentions. I may have even innocently flirted with her, if truth be told. I liked being fussed over. She was the kind of woman every man should fall in love with, the kind of woman all good men deserve.

The *tej*, that strong honey wine, mead by another name, I think, rapidly went to my head. The room glowed warmly. I unwisely attempted humor at the expense of your new home, Madison. I said, raising my glass of wine, that I hoped you two would have the *constitution* for it. I laughed out loud. Then I had to explain my failed jest. A joke that requires an explanation is no joke, I'm told. My witticism was a play on James Madison, the father of our constitution. Elaine giggled out of politeness. You shook your head and turned to another topic. But I wasn't the only one under the influence of the drink. You began to speak of your work despite Elaine imploring that there be 'no shop talk, please.' I don't even remember what you were going on about. The usual, I suspect. I do, though, recollect that you were so enraptured by your own oration, so engrossed by the words exiting your mouth, that you hadn't noticed the waiter standing over your shoulder repeatedly asking—in louder and more forceful terms—if you wanted dessert. Ultimately the poor man exhausted his patience and left. Elaine and I laughed heartily.

I was pleased with Elaine, but I was also pleased with how you spoke of your new role and the future. You talked of your plans and your dreams. I was gratified to see you interested in administrating and building a world class program in the Midwest. I was happy that your obsession with MWI was no longer all-consuming. You spoke as if you now had other interests. I smiled and mentioned that we were soon to be competitors. You said that you hoped we could be friendly competitors.

We talked about the past as well as the future. I told Elaine that I'd heard you were once a pretty good baseball player. Elaine said that she'd heard the same thing, but you wouldn't talk about it. You said that there was nothing to talk about. All that was a lifetime ago, you said.

I wanted it on record that I considered it a privilege to work with you. It had been my enormous pleasure and honor. You would be missed by everyone at the university.

Because of the wine I quipped that you might find yourself famous. And I laughed that one day Elaine could write your biography.

Adventure awaits, I said. A wife and a career. It's all very important work. Can family and fame be far behind? I asked. I wished you both all the best. Elaine promised to take very good care of you. You promised to take care of Elaine. You thanked me and said that I would always be your mentor. I said that I hoped you considered me your friend as well. I wished you both every success in your new lives.

But I find that I am repeating myself.

I digress.

Ψ

MY LIFE REVOLVES around test results. I test; and then I evaluate the findings. It is how I make a living and how I make sense of the world. It's my *modus operandi*. Results inform. And information changes everything.

Elaine and I sit together, silently and uncomfortably, awaiting Dr. Mandelbrot. He forces a weak smile upon entering his office.

"Dr. Bosh, Elaine, I have the results and unfortunately they are not favorable."

We both exhale.

"I'm afraid there isn't anything more we can do," he says. "I'm sorry."

After years of trying and hoping, after months of testing and waiting, all the appeals have been made; the final verdict is in.

"I'll *never* be able to have any children, then?" asks Elaine.

"I never say never," says the doctor trying to walk the line between upbeat and truthful. "After all, life is a great mystery, isn't it? That said, in my experience, however, successful pregnancies in cases such as yours do not occur. Again, I'm very sorry."

"And there's nothing more you can do? Nothing more we can do?" she begs.

"I'm afraid not," says the doctor.

Elaine hangs her head and utters a barely audible "uh" or "ah." I can't make out the vowel. I suppose it doesn't matter.

"Thank you, doctor," I say, standing and shaking his hand. "Come on honey. Let's go home." I help her out of the chair. She is numb.

Driving back to our big, empty house in Shorewood Hills we do not speak. Alanis Morrisette's unironic *Ironic* comes on the radio. I switch it off.

Elaine is one of many concurrent worries. My small unit, I balk at calling it a department, at Chamberlin Hall is at a critical juncture. For the past seven years I have been player-coach and cheerleader for the MWI cause. I have traveled the world promoting our agenda. I have given more interviews than I can count. At first, due in no small measure to the notoriety of my paper, it was relatively easy to spread the message. We garnered a great deal of attention, received generous financial support. Now Superstring Theory and M-Theory are getting all the attention, all the resources and, most importantly, all the money. No one is interested in MWI anymore. We were promised more federal funds in Clinton's second term. I wait. I'm not holding my breath. Even though I teach only one class per semester—as stipulated in my contract—I am at work too much. The bright spot in our department, the only real measure of success so far, was the hiring and subsequent retention of Madeleine (Maddy) Tsou, my right-hand woman. She's a rising star in the field. She was recruited by everyone and she chose to work with me in Madison. Even Susskind made his best pitch for her. She's indefatigable and brilliant. What more could I ask? She has been invaluable in developing the software I believe will take our research to the next level. Now we are on the verge of our first big test. We wouldn't be half as far without Maddy.

"Deep Blue took a game from Kasparov," says Maddy. "Did you hear?"

"No, I didn't," I reply. "Been busy."

"I recognize that it is strictly a testament to brute computational force," she continues, "but the day is coming. Mark my words. You can't stop intelligence, artificial or any other."

"Let us hope," I say. "We're kind of counting on it."

Elaine begins to spend a few nights a week with her parents in Madison. I don't make an issue of it because I assume her mother is better equipped to discuss non-motherhood than am I. I don't know what to say to my wife. Anything is liable to set her off. I try not to ask what she did with her parents. Sometimes I forget. And other times I can't help myself.

"So, what kind of mischief did you and your mother get up to last night?"

"We went to the movies. *The English Patient*," she says.

"I heard it was long. Very, very long," I critique.

"It was magnificent," she says.

"I haven't seen it," I admit.

"I want a baby," she says.

"But the doctor said—"

She interrupts me. "I want to adopt a baby. I want to be a mother. I want children. I want a family. Don't you?"

You don't choose in adoptions. You are chosen. You compete against other desperate couples to be the chosen ones. It is a ghastly, commercial process. We fill out forms, write essays and make videos. We submit medical records and sit for interviews. We are told not to get our hopes up, that it may take years to find the proper match. But, as the doctor said, life is a mystery and three weeks after our dossier is complete we are selected. We are chosen. The chooser is a young, fit birth mother from Kenosha, a student at Carthage College, due in early June. We assume the fact that we are both college professors gave us a leg up. We meet her several times, face to face. Her name is Karen and she seems lovely. She is funny and smart. She wants her babies to have a good life, a life she can't give them because of her age. She wants them to have a chance. She also wants a chance for herself. She is single and trusting. She is also serious and sincere. She makes us swear on our lives that we will take good care of the children. She is having twins: a boy and a girl. An instant family. One night Elaine informs me that we will name them Victoria and Albert. I think the names are perfect. Karen likes them too.

Elaine takes a leave of absence from her courses to prepare for the imminent arrival of the twins. She makes us take a baby class. She commandeers my home office and paints it lilac. New furniture appears. Baby-proofing becomes her new mantra.

The deliveries are normal. Routine miracles, says the doctor. We watch Victoria and Albert through the long nursery window. We wave and make silly faces at them. We have to wait another agonizing forty-eight hours. Then we all sign the papers. Karen cries. So do her parents. And so do we.

It is surreal. They are ours. These tiny human

beings belong to us. We can't believe they actually let us take them from the hospital. It seems like we should have a nurse or some kind of guardian with us, at least for the first year or two. I drive from the hospital to our house slower than I've ever driven before, cursing the idiots who pass me going the posted speed limit. Elaine is unable take her eyes off the two little packages strapped into brand new car seats. Every other second I check the rearview mirror to peek at my children to make sure they're still alive.

Whenever I pick one of them up I am afraid that their head might fall off. Neither child seems strong enough to be outside the womb. I hold them so carefully, so cautiously, that my upper arms cramp because I fear the slightest movement will do irreparable damage. Elaine's parents help out as much as possible. They've been through this before. After a while I get pretty good at changing diapers. It becomes my thing. Everything else is Elaine's thing. And after about six weeks, after the initial surge of adrenalin and disbelief begins to wear off, the sleep deprivation mounts its attack. It is relentless. We are up every ninety minutes, every night. Sometimes I leave the house early to sleep at the office. I take little cat naps. It's a matter of survival. I don't know when Elaine manages to find sleep. We talk about getting a night nurse, but she decides against it. Being a parent is much more difficult than I'd imagined. I form a speculative theory that children, newborns in general, possess some kind of undetectable biological cute power that subconsciously wills us to be their servants. A baby pheromone. Elaine is too tired to laugh. They are cute, though.

Victoria and Albert begin to display individual personality traits. Albert is a thinker. Victoria is a doer.

69

Victoria beats up on Albert. Albert thinks about the beating and then cries. They each have their own crib which restricts most of the fighting to the daylight hours.

"Dr. Bosh," shouts my assistant, "your wife is on the phone. It's urgent."

On August 31, 1997 Diana the Princess of Wales is killed in an automobile accident in Paris. The world goes into shock. It is the same day my wife tells me over the telephone that our little Albert—the thinker—is dead.

Sudden Infant Death Syndrome. Most people call it crib death. The doctor at the hospital explains that they can't explain it. He rambles epidemiologically about low birth weight, disproportionately male, so forth and so on. We are not listening. Through her tears Elaine keeps repeating, "I did everything right. I did precisely what the books said to do. Always put to sleep on the back. Well-ventilated room. Firm mattress. Close to, but separate from, caregivers. I did it all. I was careful. I did everything correctly."

Victoria now sleeps in our bed, which means no one but Victoria gets any sleep. Elaine will not let her out of her sight. I do not think that it's healthy but it's only been two weeks since Albert's death. I give her time. Her obsession may not be healthy, but it is understandable. This is her time to grieve. I feel Elaine push me away, like I remind her somehow of Albert. I call her mother who offers to move-in temporarily. I spend most of my time at the office to give my wife the space and time to mourn in her own way.

I get to the lab early. Maddy is already behind her bank of computers. She gives me the bad news without so much as looking up.

"I'm sorry, Dr. Bosh," she says. And she is. I can see the disappointment on her face.

Nothing. Not a thing. It's no mistake. It won't work. She's been over the numbers all night. There's no correlation. There's no sign. I scan the read-out she hands me, but I know Maddy is incapable of making a mistake. The results are unexpected. And, like that, our promising lead fizzles. The gateway to progress slams shut soundlessly, right in my face. We will have to find another path. It will take years to get to this point again. I was sure we were on the right track. I thought we were on the verge of something big. Bad luck is exponential.

I have no idea who would be knocking on our door at this hour. The man on the other side of the threshold hands me a document and says, "Dr. Jerome Bosh and Elaine Bosh, you have both been served."

We are being sued for custody of Victoria by the birth mother.

"Karen wants Victoria back," I say to a horrified Elaine. She bounds upstairs to check on her sleeping daughter. For the first time I fear for my wife's sanity.

The next day a team of two men and one woman from the Wisconsin Department of Child and Family Services arrives to take Victoria. I call a colleague from the law department. I read her parts of the order over the phone. She advises me to let DCFS do their job. Their actions are standard protocol in child custody cases.

"The state wants to make certain the child is safe," she says.

"Victoria is safer at home than with these . . . strangers," I reply.

"I know that, but the state doesn't," she says. "It will look bad if you fail to comply. It's the way the system works. I will apply for a temporary stay. But there are no guarantees. It will be up to the judge."

"Thanks," I say, hanging up the telephone. Elaine looks me in the eyes and begins to scream.

"No! Absolutely not! You can't! You're not going to let them take her," she shrieks. "I can't lose them both. I can't."

"It's only temporary," I say. "It's the law. We have no other option."

Elaine goes upstairs to pack a bag with Victoria's clothes and favorite toys. Part of me worries that she will try to escape out the bedroom window with Victoria. After a few long minutes they descend, Elaine smothering her little daughter with teary kisses. We both give her one last long kiss before handing her over. We tell her that we love her. Victoria cries all the way to the waiting van.

The judge decides that, until all the facts have been sorted, little Victoria is best served by remaining in the state's custody. My law colleague calls in a favor and retains the best child custody attorney in Wisconsin—Thomas Gold.

"What you have to understand," Gold says, "is that every state has its own idiosyncrasies. For instance, if we were down in Illinois your daughter would never have been removed. The birth mother would have no right to sue. After forty-eight hours the papers are signed and the adoption transaction becomes indissoluble. Once a woman in Illinois has signed and the two days have passed that's it. She has no recourse. But here in Wisconsin the law is different; it's trickier here. Wisconsin law provides the birth mother with six months to change her mind about the adoption, providing that she has reason to believe that the adopted child is somehow threatened or in a dangerous or otherwise unhealthy environment."

"But she's not—"

Gold interrupts Elaine. "I know Victoria is not in a harmful environment. I know it, you know it, Karen and her parents know it, the judge probably knows it too," he continues. "It does not, however, preclude her right to demand custody. And that's the point here in Wisconsin, that's the legal basis."

"So what does this mean, then?" I ask.

"It means you let me do what I get paid to do. You let me get your daughter back," he says.

"But when? How long will it take?" asks Elaine. "Victoria is so little. First she loses her brother, now she loses her home. She's probably terrified."

"Don't worry about your daughter," he says confidently. "They take very good care of the little ones. And, I am confident, a child Victoria's age will have no recollection of these unfortunate events."

"But how long?" she asks again.

"That's difficult to assess at present. To be honest it depends how good their attorney is," he starts to chuckle and changes his mind. "They could drag this out for a very long time given the indeterminate circumstances surrounding Albert's death. I'm sure it won't come to that, but I want you to be prepared for the worst. We will win. I will get Victoria back for you, but it may take some time.

"I'm sure if I could talk to Karen," says Elaine, "I could explain. I could get her to understand that there was nothing we could do."

73

"As your attorney I strongly advise against that. In fact, I don't want you to discuss anything concerning the case or the period leading up to the death with anyone. Is that understood?"

"She didn't even want the children," sighs Elaine. "She wanted her youth. She wanted to live instead. She gave them up, voluntarily."

"Her parents are attached to the action," says Gold. "They declare and affirm that they will help care for Victoria. Maybe they have convinced their daughter that she made the wrong decision. Maybe they want to raise the girl. Maybe they are the ones who've changed their mind."

I make a few phone calls from my office and then get in the car and head east toward Lake Michigan. It takes me about two hours to reach the campus of Carthage College.

My sleuthing doesn't take long. The campus is tiny relative to Madison. They can't have more than two thousand students, I think. I see her. Or I see someone who I think is her leaving Tarble Hall. I follow closely and catch up to her in front of a chapel.

"Karen. Karen. Is that you? It's me, Dr. Bosh. Jerry," I say.

"Dr. Bosh? What are you doing here? I don't think you are supposed to be here. Are you supposed to be here?" she asks.

"No. I don't know. To be truthful, I don't know what I'm doing here. Since Albert's death I don't know what I'm doing," I stammer.

Karen looks healthy and strong, like any other college co-ed. She almost looks happy.

"I'm sorry, Dr. Bosh, but I really should be going. I've got class," she says.

"A minute. Give me just one minute," I beg. The speech I wrote in my head during the drive disappears. I don't know what to say to change her mind. I start to stammer again. "I had to see you. I had to speak with you. I couldn't let this continue without hearing your side of it. This is killing us. Elaine is a mess. You have to know we didn't have anything to do with Albert's death. It wasn't our fault. You have to believe that."

"I'm sorry," says Karen.

"We are too. And we know you love Victoria and only want what is best. But we love her so, so much. You have to know that we'll take good care of her."

"I know that," she says looking at the ground. "I know you are good people. I'm sorry. There's nothing I can do."

"What do you mean there's nothing you can do? You can stop all this," I say, almost shouting. "That's what you can do. You can end it."

"I can't," she says softly.

"Of course you can. Tell me what I can do. And I'll do it."

"There's nothing you can do. There's nothing anyone can do," she says. "Albert is dead. You can't change that. I have no choice. I'm sorry."

She gathers herself after her little speech. Her countenance changes, it becomes more severe. She apologizes again without emotion and then walks away. I feel heavy, like I can't move.

After eight weeks of court dates and depositions, Elaine can no longer take it. She gives up.

"For the sake of Victoria, for the sake of us all," she says. "It's all too tragic to prolong," she mutters to no one.

She asks me to call Thomas Gold and drop our

opposition to the change in custody. Gold asks me if I feel the same. I tell him that I want my wife to be happy. And anyone can see that she is not happy. He counsels us to think it over for a few days before doing anything definite. Elaine does not waver.

"It wasn't meant to be," she says.

"We could try again," I say. "We're young. There are other options."

"No, not for me," she says. "I'm done."

My poor wife, I think, consigning herself to childlessness, like her beloved Austen.

I read in the paper that a woman in Des Moines gave birth to healthy septuplets. I take the copy to work and hope that Elaine doesn't see the news.

The snow today falls in clumps. It sticks to the trees. It covers the rooftops. We've gotten used to the long, white Wisconsin winters. I convince Elaine that getting out of the house would be good for her. We decide to take in a movie. She chooses *Titanic*. It's dreadful. And too long. She loves it. She cries. On the way home the car radio plays the annoying and overplayed *MMMBop*. I change the station and smile at my wife. And still the snow falls.

Ψ

My first impression, and one which remains to this very day, was that, apart from your commanding intellect, you possessed a most happy countenance. It was many, many years ago; a lifetime ago, in fact. It was at that dreadful party at school, unfortunately arranged by the Graduate Student Committee for Socialization. I noticed you across the room, where you were holding, but not imbibing, a glass of light red wine; there was a look of amused perplexity on your face, due in no small measure, I am sure, to the pitiful scene arrayed before you: a roomful of inebriated, all too awkward pedagogues. I approached you. We talked. I noted a reserved confidence beneath the sincere wit of your words. There was no sense that you were adapting your conversation to suit my taste. We shared an immediate natural and rare ease in each other's company. You asked questions. The dialogue only became about you when I directed it as such. I was agreeably distracted. You displayed a virtuous, emotional depth I had not beheld in a man before. We talked for hours. You were most delightful and I was most delighted. Our initial conversation, those fleeting, enchanting hours, and that first moment our eyes met, was all the courtship either of us required. Love at first sight, indeed. And at the close of the night—gallantry incarnate—you asked for the pleasure of my company at a future time of my choosing. As God is my witness, I would have married you then and there. You even kissed my hand, ever so lightly, when we parted. I floated back to my residence and spent a pleasant night in pensive meditation. In my dreams I was yours.

And you were mine. It was fated to be. We were very much in love, weren't we? The day we were married was the happiest day of my life, uniting the best blessings of existence. Everything was perfect. You were perfect. Oh, and the honeymoon. Our honeymoon. Rome. You took me to glorious, eternal Rome for our *luna di miele*. That first month of marriage when there is nothing but tenderness and pleasure according to Samuel Johnson. Ah, Rome: the Coliseum, the Trevi Fountain, the Sistine Chapel, the Spanish Steps—poor, young Keats. Rome: honking horns and operatic confabulations, hills and catacombs, a city so alive amidst so much death. I led you around to dark churches in search of hidden Caravaggios. You fed me forkfuls of gnocchi. And we spent a most agreeable amount of time in bed. My happiness was indisputable.

Back in Wisconsin you cheerfully labored constructing your research empire; you built walls and relationships, raised roofs and money. You were in high spirits. You seized the reins like you had been waiting for the opportunity your entire life. You were always in charge, determined, and confident; nothing fazed you. You ran your department like the captain of a ship. An apt metaphor since you were embarking on a great scientific journey, weren't you? You set sail through uncharted mathematical seas for speculative lands. When you announced that Madeleine Tsou was going to join you I had little idea what that meant, but you beamed like the polestar. You were excited and full of purpose and I was happy to be on board. In the middle of your unprecedented voyage, buffeted by mighty rogue waves and stormy skies, you were undaunted; you stayed the course. And in the midst of it all you were tranquility itself.

My university department, the literature division, was quite contrastive however. Whereas yours was replete with teamwork, camaraderie, and purpose; mine was pitted and pocked with petty personalities and wearisome drama.

Despite the innumerable demands on your time and resources, you were a caring and attentive husband; our lives were wonderful; but we wanted more. I desired motherhood and you fatherhood. Years flew by without a notice.

Our futile efforts at creating a family took its toll. When my disposition soured noticeably, you remained steadfast in your devotion, undoubtedly guessing at the nature of my agitation. If anything your attentions became more considerate; your solicitude was touching, but, in the end, ineffective.

My perturbation increased and led to a rather embarrassing and unfortunate incident that was the talk of the literature department and later became the talk of the entire university. At issue was the curriculum of another instructor. I took public offense at various works on his syllabus. I judged that he was not giving women their due respect. It was childish. I placed value on an inconsequential matter; I infused the issue with an importance with which it never should have been burdened. In colloquial terms, I snapped. I was cruel and belittling. I behaved shamefully. He, however, to his credit tried to remain composed; though he was most indignant and not without good cause. But I was relentless. His silent agitation increased to the point at which he began to cry. He was speechless. I made that poor, hapless man—a middle-aged husband and father of four— weep uncontrollably and without recourse in front of his friends and colleagues. His tears, quite visible, did nothing to mollify my rage. It was important that I destroy him; that he bend to my will. Poor, poor man! The sordid scene came to a rather unsatisfactory conclusion when I stormed out of the room threatening him with emasculating violence should he not capitulate to my demands. Predictably the incident reached the university's highest bureaucratic levels. An investigation was launched. The opinion of the inquiry committee was that I had created a hostile work environment and was subject to immediate removal. As you well know, this development did not have a favorable effect upon my temperament. And yet your support was constant. You took it upon yourself to speak with the president of the university and shortly thereafter the entire episode was quietly forgotten. I never dared ask you what was said in that conversation. If you had not interceded, I may have lost my appointment and my career. You saved me from my own despicable conduct. You saved me from myself. Lamentably, it was not the only time.

Your clemency extended to my parents. They practically moved in with us during the winters. And, oh, the fleeting Wisconsin summers and all those chaotic weekend barbeques in the Turing backyard, my father in his 'Kiss the Chef' apron, passing around tepid cans of beer, and my mother trying to make everyone feel a little less uncomfortable on tumbledown lawn furniture. And all those people, neighbors and relatives, who you didn't know and did not wish to know. Children were everywhere, screaming and running. It must have been dreadful for you. Yet you never complained; you never expressed the slightest discontent. But you could not have been enjoying yourself. That was too much to ask, even of you. You chatted amicably. You pretended to enjoy food that was invariably under- or over-cooked. You endured. And you did it all for me. Your manners and unwavering indulgence did not go unrecognized or unappreciated.

One sweltering summer Saturday stands out amongst the others. You, however, may not recall the principle event. My father had filled the little wading pool for the children. In a rather unfortunate, if polite, charade of musical chairs you landed the seat closest to the pool. You hapless thing. You were splashed endlessly, but not a word of complaint escaped your lips. It wasn't your stoicism that made that Saturday memorable; it was your action—more precisely your reaction. My cousin's toddler was attempting to join her siblings who were playing in the shallow pool. She slipped and fell face first into the water. Swiftly and deftly you reached into the pool with one hand and plucked her out before she had time to sink to the bottom. You held her aloft, suspended and unharmed, swimming in the air like she could fly. The can of beer in your opposite hand had not lost a single drop in the excitement. You calmly handed the two year-old to her frantic mother and graciously, but modestly, accepted congratulatory applause from us all. I was terribly proud of you at that moment. I recall considering my

81

improbable happiness and realized, most propitiously, that I was wed to my hero.

Sorrow came.

The most gut-wrenching sorrow came in those two tiny packages. In expectation of enjoyment we were dealt the cruelest blow, weren't we? Those little angels, the answers to our long nightly prayers, were to be the fulfillment of our family. We were supposed to live happily ever after. That was the vision. It was me. I deserve the blame. If there is fault, it lay with me. I pushed to adopt. Through the blindness of my own head and heart I convinced you that we would not be complete without the music of children playing in our home. You wanted me to be happy, but I was already so happy, wasn't I?

And then the sun rose on that awful morning and I made that horrible, most wretched discovery. I called you in hysterics. Albert was dead. I felt as if I was dying too. You took control. You told me to concentrate on Victoria. You calmed me down and raced home.

The service for Albert was a blur. I know that I was present, physically present, but I do not remember much more. It is an amnesia most welcome. You must have made all the arrangements on your own.

I awoke from the most horrific nightmares. You wiped my brow and stroked my head, reaching around Victoria, until I was able to return to sleep. You were so tender.

Gradually I recognized that my situation, our situation, was grievous, but not hopeless. We were still blessed with Victoria. We were still a family.

And events took an even more perverse turn. Karen and her parents sued us for our baby girl.

82

I remember you were prepared to battle to keep her in our home. You could see what it was doing to me; you could see that I was being destroyed, eviscerated. You were brave and bold, but I spied the fear in your eyes when I walked up the stairs to prepare Victoria's things. You were afraid I would do something imprudent, something criminal, weren't you? That was the one and only time I have ever seen you afraid of anything. Escape, however, was not my plan. I wept for two straight days. You never left my side. You stopped working; you stopped everything.

You spoke to the lawyers. You made plans for the hearing, worked day and night on strategy, prepared for any and all possibilities. You did all that and you saw to my needs too. You made certain I was not alone. Small heart had I for socializing, nevertheless you made it your crusade that I was looked after. I wondered how you could be so strong.

Through it all you never made me feel guilty, though I audibly blamed myself. Sometimes I wish you had. It would have been easier to deal with. I was mercurial. I stayed with my parents for days without calling. There were occasions on which I was almost ready to sink under the agitation of the moment. I was lost. I required all the reasonings, and soothings, and attentions of every kind that you could give. And yet you kept giving.

Later, years later, I learned about your Carthage trip to talk to Karen. You battled until the very end, didn't you? You would have kept trying forever had I not wearied of the hostilities. My knight, you would have done anything for me, fought anyone. And, for all that, you listened in perfect silence as I told you that it was time to give up the campaign. You could see the surrender in my eyes. You knew the limitation of your own powers too well to attempt more than you could perform with credit.

I was your wife and partner, no more, no less. Perhaps it was my role to play. As the bard said 'all the world's a stage and we are merely players.' It was my destiny. Whether or not I was there for you shall forever remain unresolved in my mind; but there is no question that you were there for me, whenever I needed you, always, my protector, and, always, my one true love.

Ψ

"PROFESSOR, YOU ARE being intentionally contrary," says the pretty brunette coed with a wink.

"I assure you—I assure each and every one of you—that my statements are apodictic facts backed by years and years, and reams and reams, of data. This is no parlor trick set to impress. No smoke and mirrors to create illusions. This is quantum mechanics. This is the way the world works," I say with as much gravitas as I can muster.

"Now you are being intentionally provocative," she smiles.

All of a sudden I am middle-aged.

The coed is young enough to be my daughter. If I had a daughter.

My *Introduction to Quantum Mechanics* seminar has been one of the most popular classes on campus for years. I like teaching. I didn't think I would. There's a voyeuristic pleasure in watching young minds at work. They're like funny, little, costumed, talking rats trapped in a maze. Some of them will be fortunate and manage to find the exit. Most of them will lose their way. They take my class because they think I am amusing, an entertainer, a clown, and that I am an easy grader. They

85

are not far off the mark.

"This whole alive or dead at the same time thing. The guy's imaginary cat. The electron is here *and* there. I don't buy it. You say the math works. Okay. You say that it has been tested. Okay again. That doesn't mean the current understanding of quantum mechanics is correct or complete. There has to be another answer. I'm sorry, but something either is or it isn't. You can't have it both ways. No way can it be right. There is no way a physical thing can be in two places at once. It just isn't possible," says one of my rodents. He wears his baseball cap in my classroom, backwards.

"Why is it not possible?" I ask.

"Because it doesn't make any sense. It isn't logical," he responds, overly proud of his reply.

"Who are you?" I ask brusquely and then wave him off. "I don't mean your name. I mean who are you? What are you made of? How have you come into existence?"

It's a loaded series of impossible questions that few undergraduates would even attempt to answer in front of an esteemed professor and the other students. After he splutters for a second or two, I continue.

"You didn't spring into existence from Zeus' head, did you? No, I didn't think so. You weren't assembled from unknown materials by some alien race. You aren't a ghost, are you? No, that's not it. You, sir, and every one of us, are made of ordinary matter. And in this room of scholars, this hall of learning, I am willing to bet that we (being as educated as we are) are all in agreement with science when it informs us, without exception, that matter can never be destroyed. We know that much surely. We believe that that is not only possible, but it is a fact, as real as it gets. Agreed? Good. Yes, it's elementary. Where then did the matter to create you come from? If matter cannot be destroyed, the matter that is you must have come from past matter. Yes? Part of you might have been a piece of Socrates or Caesar. Part of you might have been from Krakatoa. You might contain atoms from the age of the dinosaurs, maybe atoms that were miraculously spared from becoming coprolite. Do you know what coprolite is, young man? It's fossilized dinosaur shit. Yes. Congratulations, you might be all this and more. So I ask you again, sir, who are you?"

It's not fair. Most of the class is smiling if not laughing outright. The student goes dumb. So I keep talking.

"Verity can appear illogical. This is why some of us become scientists. This is why we test our ideas. Nature shows her cards only when we go 'all in.' You must be careful when you use the word impossible, young man. Improbable, yes. I will give you that certain events are unlikely, even improbable, but that doesn't mean they cannot happen. They are less likely, yes. Impossible, no. And once you allow the notion of probability through the door, the impossible becomes possible. But do not recoil in fear class, because by embracing probability you will find your way to a better understanding of quantum physics. This will make the quantum world easier to conceptualize and navigate."

I pause as if waiting for applause. No one claps. I continue.

"The fact that we are here, the fact that any one of us is here, discussing physics no less, is improbable, is it not?" I ask.

A student in the back declares, "No more improbable than us being somewhere else."

I can't help but smile. James Maxwell is the

student's name. He will make it out of the maze.

As an early fiftieth birthday present my wife arranges a romantic getaway to Aruba. Four nights and three days. Elaine had always wanted to go there. Escaping Wisconsin in December is a gift to us both.

The island country of Aruba in the Netherland Antilles, seventeen miles off the Venezuelan coast, averages about three inches of rainfall during the month of December. It is pouring rain, cats and dogs, when our plane lands. We eclipse the three inch mark on our first night. And it just keeps raining. No long walks on the beach. No poolside drinks. No fun in the sun. We walk through the streets of Oranjestad dodging puddles and raindrops. Locals beckon us from every doorway. *Bon bini*, they shout. We try to make the best of it. I consider buying a box of Cuban cigars and smuggling them back to Madison. I realize that I can't tell a real Cuban cigar from a fake one. I come to the conclusion that I'm being sold second-rate tobacco from Costa Rica or the Dominican Republic wrapped in Cuban bands. The salesman sees my hesitation, says something in Papiamento to his friend behind the counter and then cuts the asking price in half. Now I am certain I'm being duped. I don't buy the cigars. I decide that I don't really like cigars anyway.

At night we visit the casino in the hotel. There is something soothing about sitting at a roulette table watching the ball spin around the wheel before losing my money. I don't expect to win, so there's no pressure, no expectation to thwart. On those rare occasions when my number comes up, and I win, I get that unmistakable frisson of the improbable. That's my payoff. Elaine doesn't gamble, but she likes to sit next to me and watch the action. She thinks roulette is a ridiculous way to spend money. She likes to make fun of me when I play. I enjoy her ribbing. And I like to have her next to me.

"Fifteen, black," announces the croupier.

"Oh my God, I had a feeling it was going to be fifteen," says Elaine.

"You've got to tell me if you have a hunch. I would've played the number. Next time let me know, okay?" I say.

"Okay, I'll try."

"Thirteen, black," he drones, gathering up all the losing chips.

"Honey, you're not going to believe me, but I had a feeling that it would be thirteen," whispers Elaine.

"Seriously? I asked you to tell me if you got a feeling."

"The sensation wasn't as strong as it was the first time, so I didn't think it was working. I didn't want you to play the wrong number on my account," she explains.

Two elderly women ask politely if they can join us at the table. I stand and arrange the chairs and help them get situated. They introduce themselves and begin to talk with Elaine. I get back to my stack of orange chips just before the ball starts rolling. I manage to place a few hasty losing bets.

"Eleven, black," says the croupier.

I look at Elaine and she mouths that she knew the number again. Another winning premonition. I cast a fake angry face at her. I look at the board: fifteen, thirteen, eleven. The next number should be nine, right?

"Your husband takes his roulette terribly seriously, doesn't he?" says one of the old women.

"Yes, he does. He's a very, very serious man," says

Elaine. "I think that's because his job is being a clown. Really. My husband is a rodeo clown. Honest injun. Between you and me, I suspect he's compensating."

I look at Elaine and almost laugh. The women are beside themselves.

"Martha here used to be a dancer," boasts the old lady. "Oh, she was the toast of the town. Had legs like Cyd Charisse."

"I was a looker," she says. "That's what they all said. It's true. Yep, I was a looker in my day."

"Twenty-nine, black."

I lose again.

Elaine shakes her head knowingly. She shrugs her shoulders. I feel the blood rush to my face.

"I couldn't help it. We were talking. It would've been impolite. I didn't think it would happen again," she says.

"Tell me if you know the number. Even if you don't think it'll happen. Tell me, okay?" I plead. "We could be cleaning up here."

The former dancer points out to her friend that the ball has landed on four black numbers in a row. "It will have to be red," she says. "Odds are it'll be red."

I'm about to point out the statistical error of her ways, but the croupier spins the ball. I hurry to place my chips.

"Thirty-four, red."

The two old ladies coo with delight. They win four dollars apiece.

Elaine avoids eye contact with me. She knew the number. Again. I am on the verge of real anger.

"I'm sorry," she says. "But it is awfully scary."

"What is so scary?" I ask. Are you afraid we might actually win money?"

"No, it's not that. I'm afraid I've been pulling your

leg," she laughs. "And you actually thought I could predict the outcome. You. Mister Probability."

"Very funny. You're a hoot."

We decide to cash out. We wish the women good luck and head back to the room. We order room service and cuddle in bed bathed in the blue glow of the television. Rain taps on our windows.

In the morning the rain is heavier, the drops fatter. There's a long line of people waiting for taxis in front of the hotel. Someone says that the main road to the airport is flooded. People are unhappy and anxious. We check out at the front desk and join the queue.

Our driver lifts up our bags and we scramble into the back seat. His tiny cab is flashy. Baubles and beads decorate the inside. Little hula dolls dance on the dashboard. The music is loud. He has to shout to be heard. He says his name is Keven. Two Es. Even. With a K. He yells that the main road is impassable or impossible. Either way he tells us not to worry; he knows all the back roads to the airport. He appears not to worry about the weather conditions. He appears not to worry about much.

We head toward the interior of the island, away from the main coastal road and the airport. He speeds along as if the roads were safe and dry. Elaine and I nudge each other and point to the destruction the rains are causing. Fast-flowing rivers block our path. Landslides uproot small trees. Parts of the roadway are washed away. Keven, doesn't slow down. He is not troubled. Even keeled, I joke to myself.

"Might I interest you fine folks in some gorgeous marijuana?" he yells. "The best in all the country. For sure. It'll have you flying before your plane has left the ground."

"No thanks," we shout.

"Special price," he says. "Special rainy day price."

"No really, thanks," I say. "Just get us to the airport please, safely."

"Safely," he laughs. "Too uptight, mon. Now some gorgeous marijuana would—"

"No, thank you," interrupts Elaine. "Boarding an international flight with illicit drugs isn't on our itinerary," she says. "Not today."

"Right," answers Keven. "You're the boss." He goes silent for almost a minute. "Some fine Cuban cigars perhaps?"

Elaine and I both laugh without answering. Keven laughs too and turns up the music.

Maddy Tsou asks me into her office and closes the door. She tells me to sit down and then informs me that she is leaving the university. She's accepted an offer from Columbia. I start to make a joke about Superstring Theory but think better of it. She apologizes. She makes a point of saying that she still has faith in our research, but she doesn't feel that my heart is in it anymore. Of course, she is right. She says that she needs to be part of a team that believes in the work they are doing. She needs to feel the dedication, the sacrifice. She says that for some time now it's been as though I've been merely going through the motions, like I no longer believe.

"You do not care anymore," she says. "Your passion is dead."

My research is dead, I think. She is irreplaceable.

I tell her that I understand. I do not argue, nor do I try to make her change her mind. I thank her for her many dedicated years. She thanks me for the opportunity. She seems ambivalent and resolute, if that is possible. I understand her. She has discovered, as I did many years ago, that my once promising ideas and program for research are bust. We—I—have failed at every turn. The time for great discoveries has passed. My time, anyway. I ask her when she'll be leaving. I will be free to teach more classes, I think. I will miss her.

Elaine holds my hand and guides me through my favorite Greek restaurant, The Parthenon, into the spacious private party room at the back. A chorus of congratulations greets us. My wife has arranged a birthday party for me. It's my fiftieth. "Happy Birthday," she says. Near the kitchen entrance the wait staff in their black and white uniforms applauds. I survey the rest of the room. It is full of friends and food . . . and drinks. Someone hands me a glass of Roditis. On the other side of a plaster column I see my high school friend Bird. He's talking to my parents. Maddy Tsou is standing in front of the bright mural of the Acropolis. My sister and her husband Jeff are at a table in the corner sharing a glass of wine. Elaine even hired a videographer to capture the event. I count the entire physics department among the attendees. There must be fifty people here, I think, from graduate students to dear, old friends. We make our way slowly to the decorated head table. Elaine proposes a toast. It is touchingly poetic and heartfelt. My eyes start to tear so I kiss her to hide my face. Then the food arrives and we eat.

Even long after we finish eating the main meal, people continue to arrive. More food is ordered and the drinks keep flowing. The intermittent shout of 'opa!' interrupts almost every conversation. All eyes turn toward the flaming saganaki. I make my way

93

slowly through the crowd. I want to talk to everyone, to thank them all for coming. Elaine quiets the crowd for a moment. She reads a lovely congratulatory message from Dr. Susskind who was invited but couldn't make it because, as he wrote, 'I no longer travel due to persistent aging.' I talk to Bird Maldacena and his wife Joy for a long time. We throw down two or three shots of ouzo together. They drove up from Mt. Prospect in Illinois. He has an insurance practice there. They now have three children, the eldest, a boy, is a pretty good ball player, he tells me. I hug Maddy. A little tipsy, I whisper to her how sorry I am to have wasted so many years of her life. She says that she never felt one moment was spent in vain. Others hug her as well. It's as much a going away party for her as it is a birthday celebration for me. I work the entire room. I make fun of myself and my age. Every other person hands me a fresh glass of the delicious, ruby-red Peloponnesian wine. I drink and laugh a little too much.

At some point, late in the evening, I find myself sitting at a round white-clothed table staring into the camera lens of the videographer. He is asking me questions. He is trying to get me to talk. He says something I perceive as condescending to my profession. I launch into an alcohol-fueled philippic on the merits of physics in general and the beauty of the Many Worlds interpretation in particular. I am indignant. I am incensed. I am drunk. There is some sort of commotion behind me, but I will not be silenced. I will speak my mind to this barbarian. He abruptly leaves, but the camera remains. I continue my tirade. I will not be silenced. I will be heard. They will listen.

I feel paranoid walking into Chamberlin. I try to shake the feeling. I am not suspicious by nature. My TAs and staff are huddled around a monitor. "Play it again." They laugh until they see me.

"It's YouTube," one of them says making way for me to see.

It is me on the screen. It's from my party at the restaurant. I am obviously drunk. I am angrily slurring something about being the Don Quixote of physics, tilting against the ignorance of mankind. I feel sick. I have little recollection of this. I am about to tell them to turn it off when there is a flash on the screen. Behind me, as I am ranting and raving, two waiters simultaneously ignite their frying pans of flaming saganaki. They shout 'opa!' at the exact same time. Surprised by the screaming presence of the other, they collide dropping the flaming pans. One order of flambéing cheese lands on a woman's head engulfing her hair. The other pan falls on an empty table and sets the centerpiece afire. People scream. The camera shakes briefly as the videographer abandons his post and runs to help. Waiters pour pitchers of water on the woman. Someone smothers the centerpiece with a table-cloth. And I keep fulminating. I do not notice the commotion behind me. I keep yelling at the camera, yelling at the world.

"Turn it off," I order.

"Right away, professor," he says. "It's already been viewed over four hundred thousand times," he adds as if I should be proud of the fact.

"They're calling you the nutty professor," says another.

"How original," I say.

"It was a really great party, though," says a third. "Thanks."

It is all foggy, like it happened to someone else. I don't remember how I got home. Some party, indeed.

Most of my television guest spots follow a familiar formula. After the introduction the host usually asks me about my work. They ask trite questions about physics. They ask if my classes are popular and if I am well-liked. Some of the interviewers dip a toe into the surface absurdities of the quantum world in an attempt at humor. I try to add value to the discussion. Then, inevitably, they roll the video which the audience has seen a million times. We all listen to me rant about multiple worlds unaware of my chaotic surroundings. The video clip ends and Jay Leno asks, "What world were *you* in?" The audience laughs. Everyone laughs.

In retrospect I almost lost my tenured position at the university because of that YouTube video. It also saved my career. At first I was reprimanded and threatened. But my celebrity made my classes more popular than ever. The video took on a life of its own. I was everywhere. I saw my face on the news. I was the butt of late-night television jokes. People couldn't get enough. I was asked to do interviews and commercials. Reporters roamed the campus. The school eventually saw the potential for positive exposure. I was too popular to force out. They decided to allow me to stay. They decided to leverage my popularity for profit. They did, however, take away most of my research staff and space, which was just as well since I was on the road so often. I became a household name—the Nutty Professor of Wisconsin.

According to recent statistics, the video has been viewed more than thirty-five million times. It is one of the all-time leaders on YouTube. I fear it is my legacy.

Ψ

MAN, HAD I known your birthday party was going to change my life I would've brought you a present. I would've baked a cake. You know what I mean?

And to think after all this time we've still never officially met. After, I mean. Weird, right? It's crazy how strangers can share one moment in time, the same screwy intersection of events, and be changed forever, but in totally different ways, you know what I mean?

It was your wife, man. She's the one I should thank. She hired me. I doubt she even remembers my name. Forgot it as soon as she wrote out the check, I'll bet. To her I was just the hired help, someone to record your big birthday bash. Ooh, the big five-oh! An event that must be captured for posterity. A record must be kept. A faceless videographer, that's all I was. Window dressing. Maybe that's all I was then, but that was then, right? A lot has changed. Today, Bernie friggin' Soares writes the checks, and I write 'em big, you know what I mean?

I had left college under, shall we say, less than ideal circumstances, I'll admit. I was going to be a film-maker, man, a director. I was going to make movies, be another Spielberg. The next big thing. But first my parents made me promise to get my degree, so I enrolled in college and started paying my dues, so to speak. It was boring as all hell. You wouldn't believe how dull. I mean, come on, it was Wisconsin after all, and a tiny church college in Wisconsin at that. Man, I couldn't wait to hit the coast and make it big. But at the time the parents were holding the purse strings. So I went to class on occasion and studied when I had to. For a while, anyway.

Even in the crazy church schools, even at Carthage, man, kids get drunk and have sex. You can't stop it. It's hormones, man. I wasn't the only one, you know. It helped to kill the time, know what I mean? But then my girl got pregnant—with twins, no less. I was nineteen. I had no clue. I had no friggin' idea what to do. There was no way I could be a father, that much I knew. I was going to be a film-maker, man, a motion picture director. The next big thing. Funny, my parents made me go to a small school because they were afraid of the influence a big campus like U of W would have on me. There's your irony, man. I showed them, right?

And so I ran. I mean, I didn't really run, but I ran away, you know what I mean? I fled the scene. The scene of the crime, so to speak. I couldn't face her, the mother. There was no way I could tell my parents what had happened. So I just dropped-out. I told my parents that college wasn't for me. It wasn't working. I told them that I fully understood the consequences of my decision. But I didn't say anything to the girl. I was afraid to talk to her. Man, I was scared. I was nineteen. And one day I was just gone. I disappeared, if you know what I mean.

At first I went to Milwaukee. I didn't have the money or the resources to get to New York or LA. I worked a lot of jobs, a lot of crappy jobs. Jobs I deserved, you know what I mean? For a long time I was really down about how I handled things. That kind of thing hanging over your head, day and night, is brutal man. I couldn't think about anything else. I was split between wanting to be this big deal movie director and wanting to go back to school and take care of Karen and my kids, you know, do the right thing. There were moments I pretended I could do both. You know what's weird about being pulled in two opposite directions? It keeps you from moving. I was stuck, man. So I stayed in Milwaukee. I stayed way longer than I should have. I bounced around the city afraid to make a decision. I took any work I could get. I worked part-time in a photo hut, man, for seven years. I fooled myself that I was still in the business. My career was developing, I joked to myself. But it was pathetic. I was pathetic. I wanted to call my parents to tell them that I was okay, but I didn't. I was alone most of the time. I acted like a fugitive. I was afraid to get close to anybody, like I'd contaminate them with my bad luck. At the diner I used to eat at there was a girl. I think she liked me. She once gave me free cake. But there was no way I was going to date again. Ever. I didn't feel I had the right to get close to anyone. That's how I felt man. Later, I bought a camera and took photographs when I wasn't working, to record life, my life. It wasn't a happy time for me but I felt I didn't deserve a whole lot of happiness, know what I mean? Like I had made my own bed, so to speak. But, no matter how miserable you are, the days and years roll by, don't they? And finally, bit by bit, time made me start to forget the pain I'd caused.

A private detective my parents hired found me at my apartment. The first two times he knocked on the door I hid in the bathroom and wouldn't answer. I thought it might be Karen's dad. The detective drove me back to Madison the next day. It was time. It had been long enough. I was tired of fighting myself, know what I mean?

So I went back to Madison to kill my dreams, man, once and for all. I was thirty. I had spent a decade pretending I would one day miraculously be something, be someone else. I was fooling myself. I was nothing and had nothing. I was a friggin' bum. My parents, though, were great. I was still their little boy. They were just happy I was alive, I think. They treated me like I'd just been rescued from a cult. I took advantage of it for a while, but I didn't tell them the real reason I quit school and ran away. I couldn't.

One day my dad found my camera and said that I should try to earn money with it. It would've killed him if I'd said no. And I didn't have anything else, did I? Limited prospects, one might say. My mom said my photos were beautiful and tragic and sad. You should take more, she said. You have a gift, she said.

My parents bought me a video camera. They were so excited. I remember it cost them a lot of money. Probably more than the private detective cost. They started to recommend me to their friends at church and work. That's how I became a videographer. I worked weddings, parties, anything. Shit, I was in my thirties and living with my parents, man. I took any gig I could. I owed it to them if nothing else. I called myself BS Productions, an inside joke. It was depressing more than anything. I was a film-maker but not a film-maker, you know what I mean? I was a mercenary, a sad, failed, lonely mercenary. Sometimes I would post short videos I shot to YouTube. It was all I could do to keep from going crazy.

100

Your party, your fiftieth birthday party, a party for a professor, changed everything, didn't it? It was at that Greek place. I can't remember the name of it. The food was good, man. One of the perks of being a working guest. It was just another job to me. Your wife was real nice. I remember that. All those other friggin' college people, though—smug teachers and giddy students—that was hard for me. It reminded me of what could have been. But it was too late for me, know what I mean? I could have been one of you. You were like aliens, though, from a different caste. I thought of Karen and wondered if her life had been ruined as badly as mine. I hoped not. I certainly hadn't made it any better.

I was told to shadow you and record your interactions with your guests. To tell you the honest truth, it was pretty boring stuff. Chit-chat, mostly. By the way you were drinking I think you were probably bored too. I worried I wouldn't have enough footage to put together a decent narrative.

A couple of times, though, I saw some life peek through. You were talking about baseball with some little guy and his wife. The wife wasn't too happy, but you and the other guy were in your own world man, talking about your glory days. It would have been a pretty friggin' pathetic scene if I hadn't thought to zoom-in on your face. I captured the happy eyes of a child when you spoke. They were sparkling man.

The other time you were talking to some woman, more like consoling her. She was sad and you were trying to cheer her up. I didn't catch the conversation just your reactions. It was like she thought she'd done something bad to you and you were trying to explain that it wasn't her fault. Man, it was touching. And it played better without the dialogue.

I knew when I asked you the question that you were drunk. Everybody knew you were loaded. But my job was to catch you in action and you hadn't moved or said anything in like half an hour. When I asked the question, I wasn't trying to rattle you. I was really interested in the answer. I was after animation, man, signs of life. And I'd always been interested in science, so I thought I'd find out what an expert thinks. But, man, did you take it the wrong way. And then, a minute or two into your crazy spiel, the fireworks began. I don't even remember putting down the camera, but, man, am I friggin' happy I did.

The party was pretty much over after the fire department arrived. Anyway, there wasn't much for me to shoot. You were so drunk you couldn't even say good-bye to your guests. I helped your wife pour you into the car. She made a joke that the 'undignified' car loading shouldn't be part of my film. I told her I'd see what I could do. We laughed.

I didn't know that I'd captured the fire and commotion until after I got home. I had to watch it a few times to believe it myself. It was, you were, hilarious. Man, it was so perfect it looked staged. The contrast between your professorial drunken demeanor and the mayhem behind you, it was classic. It had the perfect arc for YouTube. I knew I had something, something big. I stayed up all night watching it over and over and then I begin my editing. I did a little to it, but not that much, you know what I mean? Prettied it up a bit, mostly. Added an intro, enhanced the sound quality, added some music for emphasis, but mostly it's all you, man. Like it was meant to be. You were a natural. It was good, real good.

As soon as it was finished I posted it to my YouTube channel—BS Productions. Yeah, sure you have. Everybody's heard of BS Productions now, I know. But you were my big break. Man, within hours I was getting calls from everywhere. The clip was a worldwide phenomenon. It was everywhere. I watched the number of viewings climb and climb. It was beyond surreal, man. Overnight it seemed my life had changed. Oh, for a while I hid—my old MO right?— but then I began to explore the offers. They were all over the map, man. I made buckets of money immediately in advertising and airing rights. The low-hanging fruit. That whole period was a crazy, friggin' whirlwind, man. It must've have been nuts for you too, right? I remember seeing you on television like a month or two later. Sometimes I felt bad, but other times you seemed like you were having fun. I thought about getting in contact with you to talk about things, but it never seemed like the right time. I was really busy, man.

So I moved out of my parent's house, out of Wisconsin, and out of the Midwest. I set up shop in LA and hired people to work for me. People worked for me, man. Soon a major studio came knocking and offered me a script that they wanted me to direct. Yeah, that's the one. *Funny Monkey* with Jim Carey. It was huge. It grossed over $200 million. My name in the business was made. I was rich. I was a director. And it all happened so fast. There is no friggin' way on this earth I can describe the feeling, you know what I mean?

After a few years I managed to catch my breath. I flew back home to see my parents. But the real reason I went back was to find Karen and my kids. Believe it or not, I hired the same private detective that my parents had hired to find me. What a world, man.

There were times, back in Milwaukee, when I slept

on the street. Bad times. I was scared, man. A lot. But, let me tell you, that was nothing compared to the fear I felt when I knocked on Karen's door. I was friggin' terrified.

At first, when I told her who I was, she was in shock. The shock got me in the door. The shock made her overly polite. We sat in her living room and she offered me coffee. There was no one else there. I didn't know how to start so I started by saying that I was sorry. Wrong and sorry. I didn't know what else to say, you know what I mean? When you did what I did, what do you say?

The sound of my voice helped her recover from the initial shock. She got angry. She screamed at me, man. I deserved everything she threw at me and then some. I thought she was going to hit me, but she threw words instead. She called me a coward. She said I had no right to come back, no right to be here. She said we were strangers, that I was just some self-centered punk from her past. She said that I might as well be dead. She said I had no right to come back here. Now that all the hard work had been done I show up. Now. Where was I twenty years ago? Where was I when Albert died? He might still be alive, if not for me. Where was I when she had to quit school and live with her parents? Where was I when she had to work at Walmart so Victoria could get new shoes? Where was I when she started to hate her parents for making her be a young mother? What was I doing when she missed out on life? Where was I then? She yelled. And now you're here. What do you expect? What do you want? Do you want to take something else from me? I have no more to give, she said. I let her go on and on. I deserved everything she wanted to throw at me. But I had no answers for her. I had not thought about

104

answers, man. I only knew that I had to face her, to say I was sorry. That was all I knew. She calmed down a little. I thought about the dead boy, my son. I said that I thought I should leave. She said that that was probably best. I stood and told her that if there was anything I could do for her and her daughter, for Victoria, just let me know. I also said that I would not bother them again unless she said it was okay. She said that there was nothing they needed from me. Those days were gone. I said sorry, again, and turned to walk to the door. Karen said she didn't need or want my apologies. I could keep them. She just wanted her life back. She wanted me to go. I left.

One year later Victoria sent me a letter that had been written with Karen's knowledge and approval. It said that she wanted to see me. It said that I could come whenever I wanted. Man, I was on the next flight out.

Karen answered the door and let me in. She said that she had no right to stop Victoria from wanting to see me. That was her business. She was almost an adult. I thanked her. She told me that she didn't want my thanks and called out for Victoria.

Victoria, Vickie she calls herself, was probably around twenty at the time. She looked exactly like her mother did when we first met at college. Man, it was eerie, unsettling. She had a habit of closing her eyes slightly when she spoke. I have the same habit. That's one thing she got from me at least.

She was really confident and controlled the conversation. She said that she'd asked me here to see what I looked like in real life and to answer a few questions she had. That was all. I said that I'd answer everything to the best of my abilities.

She asked me why I ran away and left her mother.

I told her that at the time I was nineteen and a coward.

She asked me why I didn't come sooner.

I answered that it was due to shame and poverty.

She asked me why now, after all this time.

I said it was probably that I was no longer poor and the guilt was stronger than the shame.

After she asked her prepared questions, she relaxed and we talked for a bit like human beings. She knew all about me and my career. She called my movies lame, typical Hollywood schlock. She told me that she was a theater major in school. I told her that anytime she wanted to come out to LA she was more than welcome. Our conversation was almost pleasant, man. She was a smart, strong, beautiful woman, just like her mother.

Vickie said that it was time to go. She had a date. She moved in close and whispered.

"We can be friends, but no more. You will never be my dad. Get that into your head or you'll never see me again. Never. My mom was and is both my parents. I don't need another. It wouldn't be nice, nor would it be fair."

"I know," I said.

Victoria bounded upstairs without saying good-bye and Karen entered to show me to the door. I thanked her for the opportunity to visit but she didn't answer. I took out a check I had brought with me. I gave it to her. She gave it back and said that she didn't want my money. I said that it was for Victoria, for anything she needs. I also told her that I would see that her tuition is paid for as long as she is in school. I told Karen that I knew she would never forgive me. Some things cannot be forgiven and I shouldn't try to change that.

"I won't try to take that away from you," I said.

She started to tear up the check.

"I'll just make one out to Vickie, then. I thought it would be safer in your hands."

She put the check for $200,000 in her pocket and opened the door.

"Thank you," I said. And if she ever needs more please come to me.

Karen closed the door without answering.

Now I'm married with two kids of my own, man, and I'm still trying to make up for my mistakes. But I know that I'll never be able to completely. And I figure I'll make a few more before my time's up, you know what I mean? That's life, I guess. If I complained how things turned out what kind of friggin' person would I be? Man, I'd be somebody else.

Vickie comes out to see me every so often. She wants to be an actress. I call in favors. I try to do what I can to help her career. I haven't seen Karen since that first check. We speak only through Vickie. I send money whenever she asks.

I don't make the blockbusters anymore. It's too much work. It's a young man's game. I'm happy doing the smaller films. Once in a while I'll do a documentary, usually science-related, kind of as a pay back, you know what I mean? I also fund other scientific work. I am very charitable. It's the least I can do, man. Pass around the luck. Share the wealth, right.

And, to think, it all started with you, man. All because of you and that goofy party video. Strange, isn't it? Yeah, I took it and ran, I did the best I could, but it all started with you. You were my golden ticket, you know what I mean?

107

Ψ

ELAINE ISN'T FEELING well, again. She says that it's a
female issue so I don't ask for specifics. But it seems to
me that she's had problems for months, if not a full
year. She's always tired; she spends an inordinate
amount of time in the bathroom. She no longer eats
with her usual appetite. Her back often hurts.

"These are supposed to be our golden years," I
say. "They can't be golden if you're feeling all rusty." I
smile at her, winking at my wordplay.

"Don't be foolish. I will be okay. It's nothing.
Correction, it is something. I believe the youngsters
call it old age," she replies.

"We are not old. We're at least a decade away
from old age. We are mature for middle-age, that's all."

"I feel old," she sighs.

"Then make an appointment with the doctor. Get
checked out. They've probably got a pill for that," I
joke.

"Okay. If that will make you happier, I will. But
only for you."

"Thank you, my sweet."

Oncologists are strange beings. Ostensibly human, but

once removed. Objectivity turns them into the other. They are Spock-like. At our follow-up appointment after the laparoscopy, the doctor gives us the bad news. Elaine has stage-three ovarian cancer. The tumors are poorly differentiated. The cancerous cells have spread to other abdominal structures, specifically the uterus. He outlines the treatment, the plan of attack, the course of action. There will be surgical debulking. We will try to excise as much of the disease as we can, he says, like he was discussing removing a tree stump from his neighbor's front yard. Upon your recovery from the debulking procedure we will begin chemotherapy treatment and monitor your progress.

"Any questions?"

"How long do I have?" she asks.

"That's impossible to determine," says the doctor in robotic monotone. "Every patient is unique. There are recorded cases where similarly categorized patients have survived for fifteen years or longer. Admittedly, these cases are rare. The outcome is typically less hopeful. Slightly more than half the women in your situation succumb to the disease within the first five years."

Those almond-sized organs have been terribly cruel to her in this life.

I tender my resignation immediately. The dean tries to persuade me to take some time off instead. I point out that I am almost seventy years-old. I can't stay forever. It's time. There is no reason to quit, he says, take as much time as you'd like. He is very understanding, supportive and generous. I explain that I only want to think about my wife. I don't want anything else to get in the way. I don't want anything waiting for me. I don't want the distraction of knowing that I have a future and she does not. I am done teaching. I'm done with my celebrity. I am done being that person. I'm sorry, nothing can change my mind.

"I don't want you giving up your life for me," Elaine says.

"But you are my life," I tell her. "You always have been."

With the assistance of a patient travel agent I arrange a deluxe trip to Paris for my dying wife. We both have always loved Paris. I feel that this may be our final vacation. We depart as soon as her strength recovers after her final round of chemo. We fly first class. She enjoys the flight and the pampering. She asks where we are staying in Paris. I won't tell her. I tease her. I've booked four nights at the Ritz. It costs fifteen hundred dollars a night, but I'd spend every penny I have to purchase one extra second of happiness for her. I want her to be surprised, happily surprised. I don't speak any French, but for a week I practiced the correct pronunciation of the address so she won't know where we're staying until we pull up in front of the hotel. *Quinze, Place Vendôme*, I repeat in my mind for most of the flight. I want her to be surprised.

I help guide her into the taxi. She winces a little. I jog around to the other door and squeeze in next to her. I smile, clutch her arm and confidently say to the cabbie:

"*Quinze, Place Vendôme, s'il vous plaît.*"

"Ah, the Ritz Hotel," he says in perfect English. "Right away."

The first night we eat at a little Mexican restaurant not far from the Eiffel Tower. It was recommended by one of our friends back in Madison. It is quaint and the food is delicious. Elaine doesn't eat much. She picks and moves the food around her plate to hide her lack of appetite. We decide to walk around the neighborhood after the meal, an evening constitutional. The night air is refreshing. It's a residential area, quiet and picturesque. During the stroll Elaine notices a plaque on the wall. She informs me that Balzac lived here. She muses on the serendipity. She is happy.

The Louvre is too crowded. I.M. Pei's pyramid seems old-fashioned now. We both remember the controversy that this 'futuristic' addition once caused. It was around the time we first met. We laugh sadly thinking about how many years have passed. We move through the museum halls in desultory fashion. I look at my wife more than I do the artwork on the walls. We don't stay very long.

Paris moves at a gallop. Elaine walks slowly. The cobblestones are treacherous; the sidewalks are narrow and mined with feces. We try to make the best of it. But even the short walk from the hotel to the Tuileries Gardens is difficult for her.

The hotel is wonderful, all that I thought it would be and more. The Ritz staff is amazing. Somehow every last one of them knows the difference between guest and gawking tourist. We are treated like royalty. It is like living in our very own palace. People on the plaza snap photos as we exit. (Perhaps one day, long after they've returned home from their holiday, these shutterbugs will examine the captured elderly couple and conclude that we were neither rich nor famous.)

We take cabs around the city. We visit other *arrondisments*. We gaze at Sacré Coeur at sunset and sit in the cafés of Montparnasse for lunch. Elaine remarks how long it's been since the famous writers and artists sat where we are sitting. Generations, she sighs. We go all the way out to Père Lachaise Cemetery because Elaine wants to see the graves of Nancy Cunard and Gertrude Stein. I hold her hand as much as I possibly can. I memorize every laugh line on her face. I try to make her smile. The four days in the City of Lights passes far too quickly, just like our forty years of marriage.

Dozens of messages from around the world greet me at home. One note, from a friend at the California Institute of Technology, informs me that a recent poll of physics shows that the Many Worlds interpretation is more popular than the Copenhagen interpretation. While I was not looking, Everett had his victory over Bohr. I am almost happy for a moment, but not for myself. Most of the messages revolve around my dissertation being 'rediscovered.' My ideas are now back in vogue, the hot topic, the new big thing. Again. Physicists around the world want to pick my brain. They are waiting to hear from me. The only thing waiting for Elaine is death. I ignore the physics fuss and focus on my wife. And on the time she has left. Maddy is the only one from the outside that I'll talk to. Mostly I talk about Elaine. I confide in her. I share my fear.

"She's dying, Maddy. My wife is going to die. And there's not a goddamned thing I can do to stop it."

I see her motionless body but I like to think that she's alive, in another world, perhaps. I begin to miss her even before they close the casket. The day I bury her is the saddest day of my life. My friend, my partner, my true love is gone. The pain is now mine alone. The gravestone is made for two. Husband and Wife. Under

Wife, the marks are simple and factual:

Elaine Mae Turing Bosh
1966–2022

My side of the stone waits to be etched another day. I silently wish for it to be soon.

My misery soon becomes anger. Instead of ignoring the requests for my time and knowledge, I write insulting replies and leave angry messages to total strangers. I mock them. They are all idiots. I beg to be left alone. Maddy presses me to come out to New York. I decline with malice. My sister checks up on me and I yell at her too. For no good reason. I feel I have a right to be angry. Elaine is dead. That's enough, isn't it? Sometimes I don't know why I'm so angry. It feels like it's more than heartache. Sometimes I feel confused in unfamiliar situations. I forget that I've forgotten things. I experience short-term memory loss. I assume these symptoms are the toll of grief, the price of my pain.

My sister and her husband tell me that they are worried about me. They look-in on me frequently. Almost every day. I can take care of myself I say over and over again. I tell them to go to hell, but they persist. Somehow they get me to agree to see a doctor. He asks me silly questions. They scan my head every which way. The doctor would like to see you again, says my sister. They think they have an answer. I try to remember if I've ever had good news from a doctor of medicine. And then Dr. Kao delivers the blow, life's final blow.

"I'm afraid it's early stage Alzheimer's."

My sister starts to cry. Her husband swears under his breath.

"How soon?" I ask.

"The progression of the disease is variable. It's impossible to ascertain with any confidence," says Kao.

"There's no chance that it won't develop into full-blown Alzheimer's then?"

"No. I'm sorry. But who knows what advances the future may bring?"

"The nutty professor dying from dementia. At least there's some symmetry to it. Supersymmetry, even." I treat the news as a joke. What else can I do?

I have full-time care courtesy of my sister and brother-in-law. The girl—her name is Cheryl or Shirley—cleans and cooks for me. Sometimes we take walks. She talks to me a lot, but I don't say much in return. I grumble a great deal. Susan and Jeff visit as much as they can. My sister spends most of her time crying. I continue to get messages and requests from old friends and old colleagues. She reads them to me. I don't read as much as I used to. It's hard to do now. It makes me sad.

One of the notes she reads sounds nice to me. And the fact that it is hand-written makes it nicer. The author of the note wants to interview me about my work. He works for some magazine that I've never heard of. I tell Cheryl or Shirley to call him. I want to answer his questions. She says that I'm not supposed to grant—she uses the word grant—any interviews. Your sister's wishes, she says. I tell her that I don't give a damn what my sister says, I am going to talk to this person. After a long standoff, she nervously calls him. She hands me the phone. But the man on the other end does not sound at all like his note. He doesn't sound nice even though he is thanking me for calling. He asks about my dissertation. I say that it's been fifty years since it was written and that I buried it a long time ago. I ask him why he wants to dig up a corpse. He thinks I'm joking and laughs. He says that many people now believe my work was correct all along, that the scientific community made a tremendous blunder and ignored a major scientific accomplishment. I tell him that I have never been ignored. I do the ignoring, I say. Anyway, who cares about what people say? They are all idiots, always were. And so are you, I shout. The girl grabs the telephone from my hand. I am shaking. I don't know what came over me. I'm not proud of the way I act. I don't understand why I do it. I don't like this version of Dr. Jerome Owen Bosh. I don't like myself very much. The only thing I like, the only thing that brings me any comfort, is that my wife was spared seeing me like this—at least in this world.

Ψ

IT WAS WEDNESDAY, the fifteenth, cloudy but without measurable precipitation. The air temperature was seasonal. We had arranged our rendezvous for 12:30 at Wishbone, the campus diner. The restaurant was darker than I would have preferred. The well-worn tables and chairs were mismatched: most were wobbly, with coasters wedged-in between legs of various lengths and the checkerboard tile floor in a half-hearted effort to minimize the tottering. Large brown ceiling fans slowly circulated the conversations and the odor from the kitchen. I arrived early and was shown to a red, leather-upholstered booth by the window. There was a small tear in the fabric at the farthest corner. The stuffing had started to escape. I picked at the fleeing foam while I waited. This helped me fight the urge to pull back the dusty curtain to see if you were approaching. I must admit I was anxious about the meeting, our first. (At the time I was unable to ascertain the source of my anxiety; that realization would come much, much later.) I knew who you were certainly. Your name was well-known, almost famous, and we had corresponded via email and spoken briefly on the telephone once. Yet I was uneasy. I felt ill-prepared for our meeting and that was unlike me, both the feeling and the lack of preparedness.

I recognized you immediately, though you were much taller than I'd envisioned. You stopped next to the old cash register for a moment or two surveying the room. I waved feebly. Or at least I felt my wave was feeble. You smiled and in three long strides reached the booth and slid in across from me and started talking. I remember our conversation verbatim.

"Madeleine, Madeleine Tsou, I am honored to meet you, really honored. And thank you so much for taking the time out of your busy schedule to talk with me. I've looked forward to this for a very long time, a very long time."

Before I could reply, the waitress deposited two glasses of water and two menus on the table and mumbled that she'd be back in a minute to take our orders.

My attempt at speech was lost to her interruption so you kept talking. "You are exactly how I'd imagined. You are positively perfect."

The words by themselves bordered on the fulsome, but your smile and energy and the unbridled enthusiasm you exhibited reassured me that there was not a duplicitous bone in your body. You could not have been disingenuous if you'd wanted. You spoke from your heart, from a place of sanguine devotion.

"I knew it. I knew we'd get along. When I examined your work, I just knew that we were kindred spirits. It's like we are both on the same long journey, but we were traveling alone. Well, we've met up now, right? Have you decided yet?" you asked.

"Yes," I answered. It was the first word I'd spoken.

"Brilliant," you said, "then let's eat."

It was only later that I understood my first word, my yes—that tiny word of assent—wasn't about my lunch order. My yes was to you. My yes was the verbal acknowledgement that I would come and work with you, that I had accepted your offer above all the others. You knew that though, didn't you?

You had a BLT and fries. The lettuce was soggy. I picked at a mixed salad. We both drank water. The waitress refilled our glasses twice. You offered me some of your French fries. I declined.

You spoke of your work in almost religious terms. Not that you were on a crusade. No, it was more like you'd seen the Garden of Eden and wanted everyone else to be able to see it as well. You painted a vision of extraordinary beauty and simplicity. And then you stopped talking. You looked me in the eyes. And you waited.

I should have been nervous, at least more nervous than I was before you'd arrived. But I wasn't. I talked. And talked. I told you about my work and my dreams, about my upbringing and my fears. I told you things that I had not disclosed to my best friends. Don't ask me why I opened up like that; I would fail to find an answer. Something about you made me want to. It became supremely important that you know everything about me. It was important to me.

When I was done, when I had no more to say, you leaned in and quietly said: "Thank you. You are perfect. We make a great team. Together we will unveil worlds."

"I know," I replied.

The lunch lasted for over three hours. It felt like five minutes. I did not want it to end. You over-tipped the waitress—I peeked and saw that you left her twenty-five percent—and offered to walk me back to my apartment, but I needed to be alone to process what we had discussed. A tacit agreement had been made. My life took an irrevocable turn. I needed to understand why and how it had happened. And I needed to prepare.

It was Madison, Wisconsin, but it could have been Outer Mongolia; it could have been anywhere. I find it interesting that place held little or no meaning given that our mission was to prove the existence of other worlds. In the beginning, I would have followed you anywhere. And you knew that, didn't you? Once I'd committed, I was yours.

For all intents and purposes we lived at Chamberlin Hall, didn't we? Eleven-fifty University Avenue. Those heady, early years weren't work; it wasn't a job. It was something else—a calling. Yes, a calling. We prayed at the altar of the apodictic. We surrendered to rationality. We submitted to science. And you led the way. You preached that the truth would set us free. In many ways you were our prophet.

I lived in computer code. Your faith in me was energizing. We discussed a thousand solutions to our measurement issues. We built and modified and tested and rebuilt lasers over and over. We analyzed and debated the merits of photoluminescence modulation versus photocurrent. Every promising idea was explored. Nothing was sacrosanct. And we had some early success, didn't we? Oh, the first time we were able to measure the electron spin resonance linewidth and the coherent Rabi oscillations, I thought you were going to kiss me. I don't think I'd ever been happier.

Complications were inevitable. I was prepared for setbacks. No road is without its rough patches. But you were devastated when the data showed that you

119

had not been correct. You changed. It may sound mean, but failure changed you.

I stayed at Chamberlin all night to watch the data aggregate and compile. All the other lights in the lab were off. Only the monitors illuminated the room. I knew early on that the numbers were unfavorable; the data were not what we had anticipated. When you arrived in the morning, looking like you hadn't slept all night, I didn't know what to say. I could see the disappointment on your face when you read the bad news on mine. And that was the beginning of the end.

"I'm sorry, Dr. Bosh," was all I could muster. You said nothing. You glanced briefly at the data and then you turned and left.

If you hadn't been experiencing other issues—your wife, that horrible affair with the children—I would have blamed myself for your abdication. I felt as though I'd personally let you down. I knew that wasn't the truth, but it was so difficult watching you in such pain that I didn't feel I had the right to explain. We left you to yourself. And you dealt with all that pain and adversity by withdrawing from the one pursuit, the one diversion that could have saved you. You abandoned your dream; you surrendered, slowly and cowardly. It was painful for us all.

No church—my friends called it a cult—led by a charismatic leader lasts long. And when you—our leader—stopped believing, your flock found other faiths. I still believed we were right. I still believed in the work. I still believed in MWI. I kept the faith. I just stopped believing in you. And so I planned my departure.

The YouTube video and its aftermath reaffirmed my decision. That footage, played over and over again, everywhere, felt like a public intellectual flogging. All your torment was put on display. All your promise turned to humiliation. You had become a shell of a scientist. You became an impotent performance piece. You were theater. Watching you on talk shows and game shows, I could tell you no longer believed what you were saying, but yet you continued to try and sell the idea to the public. You were like a used car salesman. And at your worst you laughed at yourself. The man I knew as a genius joined in his own ridicule. I was appalled. In my eyes you had gone from prophet to puppet. It hurt. I felt betrayed. But it also made me work harder to prove to you, and to the world, that we had been right.

I tried for years, many years, to convince you to return to the research. I kept you updated on every success, every dead-end. I asked for your counsel. You laughed off or ignored my queries. Although you were in New York often, you never had the time to sit down with me and discuss the work. You were forever too busy. There was always too much to do. You were only in town for a few hours. A quick interview and you were on a return flight. You'd call me from Madison.

And you would call. We talked. We talked often, but it was never about work. It was about life. It was small talk. When Elaine got sick we talked more frequently. You talked. I listened. That seemed to be what you needed from me at the time.

An over-weight woman carrying a dirty black plastic bag bumped into me and as I turned toward her I saw you. I recognized you immediately, even though you were sitting down facing away from the window. It was you: a thinner you, but you all the same. You were eating alone in a diner on the Upper West Side. If it hadn't been for that woman I would have passed by without ever seeing you. I practically sprinted into the restaurant.

"A creature of habit, I see," I said.

"Huh?"

"Your food. A BLT and French fries. You are a creature of habit. You ordered the same thing the first time we met, remember?" I said.

"Maddy!"

You stood and hugged me. You hadn't lost any of your height. I sat and we talked. You seemed happy to see me. I was happy to see you. We chatted for an hour. You were in the city to be on The Tonight Show. You asked me if I'd like tickets. I declined and asked after Elaine. We joked about the winters in Madison. I asked if Chamberlin had changed. You asked if I was still single.

"Married to my work, I fear," I replied.

"There's more to life than work," you said, playfully waving a fry in my direction.

I smiled and then became serious.

"What happened?" I asked.

"What do you mean?" you said.

"You. What happened to you?"

"Nothing. I'm right here," you laughed.

"You are different. You were different. You were a giant," I said.

You laughed again, but in a deeper, slower manner. "Perhaps it is you who has changed?" you said. "Have you considered that, Maddy? Maybe I have not gotten smaller, maybe it's you who has grown?"

"Together we will unveil worlds. That was what you said. That was your promise."

"I said that?"

"Yes, you did."

"I must have meant it at the time," you said. "I'm sorry that I don't remember saying it."

"I'll never forget it," I said. "I can't. I've dedicated my life to it."

"Maddy, I hope you get what you want."

"I didn't abandon you," I said. "You left first."

"I know," you replied.

You looked down at your watch, took a sip of water and announced that you were due at the studio. I offered to walk with you, but you said that you'd prefer to be alone. "It helps me prepare," you said. We hugged again, longer this time. You said that it had been a wonderful surprise to see me and I could see in your eyes that you meant it. I watched you walk down Amsterdam Avenue and disappear into a crowd waiting for the light to change.

I couldn't be angry with you. You had become somebody else. That was all. And you appeared content.

After that conversation we never spoke of work again.

And then Elaine died.

We barely said hello at the funeral. It was terrible. It was the last time we would see each other.

I had decided to attend the service at the very last minute and caught a flight from Newark that got me into Madison the morning of the internment. It was a beautiful day. The air was fresh. The sun was unusually bright. It made everything appear hyper-real. There was a visual crispness, demarcation made manifest, which accentuated object discreteness. Each blade of grass stood in proud relief nescient of its neighbor. It all remains so vivid in my mind. The serrated leaves of a large oak tree waved their fingers. The white gloves of the pallbearers floated out from dark sleeves. Tears rolled, one by one, down perfumed cheeks, and dropped to the ground, into oblivion. The glossy gold casket containing Elaine's body reflected cold light on black dirt.

There were hundreds of mourners: friends and family and others. Many of them had loved Elaine, but they were there for you. Their sadness, their support, their consolation, failed to reach you; it couldn't help. Solace was without meaning. You were in your own world. Your pain could not be shared with others. It was yours alone. You watched the proceedings without speaking, without emotion, without so much as a tear. You had nothing left.

You leaned unsteadily against your brother-in-law as the long line of mourners passed extending unheard, hushed condolences. Your sister made repeated apologies for your taciturnity. You limply shook hands without looking up, acknowledging nothing but your own isolating catatonia. I had never seen you so quiet or so defeated. Ever. It was as if you were attempting to disappear.

On the flight back home I asked the flight attendant for a whiskey. I never drink whiskey. I raised my cup and took the first sip for Elaine and the second one for you. After my third bottle, high above the hills of Pennsylvania, I thought I had discovered something poetic or heroic in your silence, a testament to your love for Elaine.

I waited six weeks and then telephoned you to ask if you'd like to come out to New York. I calculated that a change in environment would be of benefit. I didn't say anything about work. I didn't mention the research. It was a social call, a personal plea. It was a short conversation. You refused angrily. We spoke less often after that.

A few years later, with assistance from our colleagues at the University of Delft, we made the breakthrough I'd been expecting. We were finally able to reverse and capture the nanotechnology. We replicated the test, over and over, to be certain. We drank champagne. We hugged and kissed. There was circumspect mention of Nobel Prizes. We still had far to go, but I and everyone in that lab in New York City knew that Many Worlds was correct, that Everett had been correct, that *you* had been correct, and that a new era in physics had begun. I'd always thought you were right, I never doubted your ideas, but now I knew it to be true. And I wanted to shout it from every rooftop in the city. I had not been wrong devoting my life to the cause. I had been right. I knew it. My greatest regret, the only damper, was that I couldn't share the news with you. By then you were quite sick. We'd been told that you were too disabled to understand what was going on around you. I was tempted to tell you the good news myself. I wanted you to know. I wanted you to hear it from me. In the end my team dissuaded me. After all, the news might make him worse, they had cautioned. I thought: How could it be worse? But I did not call.

Ψ

"I TOLD YOU before. My name is James Maxwell. I was one of your students. Your sister Susan agreed that my visits might be advantageous for both of us," he says.

He says my sister said it was okay for him to be here, but my sister is only nine years-old so I think he's lying. She can't even cross the street by herself.

"Where's my sister?" I ask.

"At her house, I assume."

"Now my sister has her own house? Sure she does. Get out or I'll scream."

I can only see her backside. She hides what she's doing like it's some big secret. I can tell that she's drawing lines and circles, but I don't know why. I don't know who she is and I don't care. She finishes and spins around and points both hands to the whiteboard. Then she explains her artwork.

"See, I have put all the important information for the day here on the board."

I read the board. It's written for a child. I look around the room but don't see any children. I'm the only one here.

"My name is Cheryl," she reads. "Your name is

Jerome. Today is Thursday the eleventh of September, 2042. This picture, this one right here, is supposed to be the sun, because it is sunny outside. It is going to be seventy-two degrees today. Hey, maybe later we can take a little walk outside in the warm sun."

She must be an idiot, I think.

"Elaine, would you please make me some toast with a little butter and jelly on it?" I ask. You know the way I like it, not too much butter. I'm not feeling that well or I'd do it myself. I'm a little tired."

"Sure," says Elaine. "Would you like one piece or two?"

At first it's great to see my parents. It seems like it's been a long time since we've talked. There's no news so I remind them of funny things that happened when I was younger.

"Do you remember the time that Bird and I drove into the city and got so drunk we forgot where we parked the car? I called you from a payphone near Division Street at three in the morning and you two came all the way from home to pick us up. Susan was asleep in the back seat. Boy, you were not happy. I was in so much trouble. I'm sorry for that," I say.

My mom starts to cry. My dad hugs her. I hear her say that it's too difficult. She can't do it. She's crying that she's somebody's sister. She calls my dad by the wrong name and says that she can't do this anymore. I don't know what's wrong with them.

Sometimes I feel sick and tired. So tired. I stay in bed for hours not really thinking of anything. Sometimes I groan even though I'm not in pain. I don't know why I groan. I don't know if it helps. These are long days.

"I wouldn't expect you to remember me," he says. "I was one of thousands. I'm sure I didn't stand out among all your other students. And I'm older now, of course. Not wiser, but older," he laughs.

We are both uncomfortable.

"I'm sorry," I say.

"Please don't give it a second's thought. I felt . . . I feel . . . I wanted to say thank you. That's all. Because of you I became a physicist. Because of you I found my calling. Your work inspired not only me but countless others. And now your ideas are finally recognized and appreciated by the scientific establishment. You are the father of a new branch of physics. Hugh Everett III is the grandfather, but you are the father. If you only knew what a giant you are, what you've given the world. I feel I owe it to you to try, to not forget, to pay my respect."

"What'd you say your name was?" I ask.

"Maxwell. James Maxwell."

I remember teaching many young people, but I don't remember him.

A strange woman brings us both small cups of apple juice.

Elaine asks me if I'm okay.

"I'm fine. Just a little dizzy, that's all. I'll be fine in a minute."

She smiles and says okay. She writes the date on the whiteboard. I want to ask her why the date is so important to her, but I don't. I just watch her move around the room. She picks up my pajamas and takes the bedding off the bed. I don't remember her changing her clothes. I don't remember her sleeping beside me. She asks me what I'd like for breakfast. I

128

pretend not to hear her. I don't want anyone fussing over me.

"I was intimidated by you. I was scared. I was nobody. You were famous, you were smart. You were everything I wanted to be. You were Dr. Milton L. Susskind. And when you agreed to be my dissertation advisor I thought I was dreaming. You met Einstein. You knew Everett. What were they like?"

"I have no idea," Dr. Susskind replies. "How could I possibly answer that?"

"Yeah, you're right, who really knows anybody?" I say.

I've forgotten her name. The name of that damned woman who's always in my house. Her name begins quietly, like a spy's name. Ssshhh. Something. She invites miscreants into my home. She probably has wild orgy drug parties while I'm sleeping. I'm sure she's stealing from me. I don't trust her. I try to tell people that she is a thief and a criminal. No one will listen. They all pretend to listen, and then they go away.

I am not me.

Bird is nervous. He always was a little jittery. Even as a kid. It's like he'd like to go out in the backyard and throw the ball around to work off all that energy. An older woman sits next to him. She looks kind of familiar, but not really. He says that she's his wife and that they have three children, grown now. Bird is joking. He was always a jokester. I don't know why he's so nervous. He's my best friend. He always will be. Bird and the old woman do not stay long. Bird hugs

129

me at the door and the strange woman kisses me on the cheek.

She should have been happy.

I say my name. An article about me appears. It says I'm dying and that no one has seen me in years. It describes ideas and mathematics and computing that have changed the way humans think about nature. The article says that these are my ideas. Some of the things in the article are true. I don't remember a lot. And some of the things are made up, like someone pulling a prank. That's not me, I whisper to myself. People are liars. I throw the reading machine against the wall and it shatters with a dull crunch. I look at the pieces on the ground and wonder why I am so angry.

"Elaine, I still know the words," I shout. "Listen to this: If I loved you less, I might be able to talk about it more. But you know what I am. You hear nothing but truth from me."

Elaine says that it is lovely.

"Of course it is," I say. "But I remember it, that's what's amazing, don't you think? After all this time, after all these years. I remember your Austen. I remember that day like it was yesterday. The happiest day of my life."

Today I only got out of bed to go to the bathroom. I think. The day was over before it had time to begin.

"I think we're close, Maddy. I can't wait for the results. Let me know as soon as they're in. We need to process the data very carefully. No mistakes. I have a good feeling, Maddy, a very good feeling. I couldn't have done this without you. It's exciting, isn't it?"

There were two babies in my nightmare: a baby boy and a baby girl. The boy vanished into the black of the night. The girl flew away on huge paper wings. I tried to fly after her, but I had no wings, paper or otherwise. Elaine watched me jump into the air and flap my arms, time and time again. Then Elaine started to shiver from the cold. Her skin turned blue. I stopped trying to fly and tried to warm her up. I couldn't. Her tears froze on her face. I tried to help. I picked off the tears, one by one. She screamed in pain as a tiny piece of brittle flesh broke loose with every tear I tore.

I see my sister crying in the snow. She's so small. She's helpless. I ask her if she remembers crying in the snow. I remember it so well. My sister smiles at me but doesn't answer.

Everybody wants to talk to me. It's because of that stupid video. It's not me. It's the goddamned fire in the background. It's the noise. It's not me. They don't really want to talk to me. They don't care about me. It's the fire. It's the noise. I didn't know. I didn't know what was happening. Everybody wants something from me.

The world seems smaller than it used to. Am I dying?

"Your smile lit up the Paris night when you found Balzac's house. You were so happy. It was after that dinner at the little Mexican restaurant. Remember? You hardly ate a thing. It was so quiet there, in the middle of the city."

131

"I will not be afraid."

"Are you okay?" I hear.

I hide and don't answer.

I'm wasting my time. I'm wasting their time. It's a game. They are all rats. They can't learn. They won't listen. They can't see the beauty in it, the simplicity, the logic. They don't understand. They'll never get it. They are all pea-brained rats. They'll never get out.

Everybody wants to talk to me. It's because of my arm, my pitching. It's not me. It's the spin of the ball. It's the noise. It's musical. I can hear it spin. They don't really want to talk to me. They don't care about me. It's the spin. It's the noise. I didn't know. I didn't know what was happening. Everybody wants something.

She wasn't happy when I showed it to her. She should have been happy. I was proud. I figured it out all by myself. It was code. The solutions were so simple. But she should have been happy. I got in trouble.

"We had a real shot, didn't we, Bird? We were headed to state. And then Penrose pulls me. He says it's to rest me for the next game. But there was never a next game, was there? I struck out twelve in a row, didn't I? They couldn't touch me. We had a real shot. Twelve in a row. My grandfather saw it too. My grandfather was there."

I tell myself to keep my arms down before I go to sleep.

Einstein and Everett.

The horses pulling a wagon with a flag. That little boy salutes. Kennedy. On the big brown box. No one talks. No one sees me behind the bars. The wagon with the flag. The white horses. I remember.

"I can do it myself! Leave me alone!"

"Do you remember crying in the snow? Do you?"

I was scared. So scared.

Her female parts made her sad and then they killed her.

"No, that's impossible!"

"It's going to work, Maddy. We are right."

"Do you remember the time Bird and I drove into the city and got drunk?"

"My name is Bosh! Dr. Jerome Owen Bosh! You can't do this to me!"

"I remember your Austen."

"Do you remember?"

These women are trying to poison me. They watch me eat. They follow me with their eyes.

"Don't you remember?"

"We had a real shot, didn't we Bird?"

"Yes. You said yes. You said I was marvelous."

Remember?

The Ψ is universal.

Ψ

THE WAVEFUNCTION IS universal. It is a cornerstone of contemporary physics, the biggest event in science since the discovery of the quantum world. It has changed the way we look at ourselves and the universe. It has changed everything.

And they named it after you, in part. It is called the Everett-Bosh (EB) principle. I teach it—try to teach it anyway—to my university students at UWM. Yes, I've followed some of your footsteps. I also renounced research to teach. Oh, don't misunderstand me; I am not attempting to compare myself to you. That would be ludicrous. I am merely mentioning the happy coincidence.

Let me begin again.

My name is James Maxwell. Dr. James Maxwell. I was once one of your many wide-eyed, unctuous students at the University of Wisconsin, Madison. One of thousands, no doubt. I became a physicist because of you. You made me want to become a physicist. You taught me how to be a physicist. You gave me purpose. You were my inspiration.

After university I worked at Cal Tech for a number of years. I got married and raised two children:

a boy and a girl. Budget cuts threatened to reduce my research, so I began looking for other opportunities. My wife and I both missed the Midwest and when you retired from the university, I applied for the open position. Inexplicably they offered me the job. You probably wouldn't remember, but with the blessing of your sister, Susan, I visited you many times after my return to Madison. I don't think you ever once recognized me as one of your former students. Your disease was quite advanced. Nevertheless we talked. I was probably just another stranger to you, another ghost. It was toward the end. You were very sick.

This is not proceeding as I'd hoped. Let me try yet again.

A corollary to the Everett-Bosh principle makes it clear that worlds do not interact with each other because of the linearity of the wave equation. Ergo, though you, dear Dr. Bosh, are deceased in this world, you are, with certainty, still alive in many other parallel worlds. The number nears the infinite, in fact. In none of these alternate worlds would you be able to hear my voice or read these words. Such interactions are precluded under the EB principle. That being said, my methods are my own. Recording and organizing my thoughts in this way has always been an invaluable tool in my decision-making process. It may be rather un-orthodox, but I have confidence in the technique.

Last month a large publishing company offered me a considerable amount of money to write your biography. They pitched that as a physicist and one of your former students and someone who knew you personally—albeit mostly at the very tragic end—I was uniquely qualified to 'do justice' to such a great man. For the record, despite my eleventh hour visits to your home, I never claimed that I knew you personally. I have never pretended to possess any exclusive knowledge or insight. Still, the offer was made and I requested time to consider the undertaking. On one hand I think it would be an incredible opportunity to learn more about you and your work. On the other hand I would be committing years of my life to the project with no guarantee of success. This exercise, these outlining notes, I trust, will help me reach the right decision.

First Impressions

One is first struck, indeed, almost overwhelmed, by the near flawless physiognomy of Jerome Bosh. He stands well over six feet tall and his well-defined musculature and perfect posture are evident beneath his neat, tailored suit. He is much larger, more imposing, more self-assured, than most scientists. He moves with the power and confidence of a professional athlete. It is only later that I learn he was once a promising baseball player with major league potential before an arm injury ended his career. Human history is often shaped by the smallest events.

Youth

Jerome Owen Bosh was born in Chicago, Illinois in 1962. His father was an elementary school science teacher and his mother was a homemaker, which was common for their class and the era. Bosh is on record a number of times stating that his first recollected memory was that of the funeral of President John F. Kennedy. He alleges that he watched the sad event through the spindles of his crib when he was barely one year old. In minute detail he described the scene in the cramped second floor living room: silent, sad adults transfixed on the blurry images of a caisson, white horses and mourners. He invariably followed this story with the disclaimer that his memory could very well have been an anniversary, a rebroadcast, of the sad event. How could he know the difference at that age? Bosh's ego never stood in the path of logical potential alternatives.

He had a modest upbringing, perhaps best described as middle class. His family (his sister Susan was born four years after Jerome) moved to the suburbs when he was six years-old. His early student years were uneventful, despite evincing a genuine mathematical precocity. Overall, he was a very good, if not excellent, student. The relative mediocrity surrounding him undoubtedly led some to over-estimate his general intellectual gifts. There are no recorded indications or allusions to any developmental or psychological problems or concerns. It appears he had an uneventful childhood. Susan should be questioned extensively about these early events and friendships.

Teens

Bosh became a star baseball player, a pitcher primarily, in high school. Given the suburban milieu, his athletic notoriety predictably overshadowed his academic gifts and achievements. Despite the lack of attention, he graduated number two in his high school class and earned a variety of prizes, including the school's top science award. His physics teacher, a Mr. Paul Minkowski, remembered him fondly as 'a hesitant and confident savant.' An interestingly revealing, if some-what awkward, description. His best friend at the time (and lifelong friend), Steven 'Bird' Maldacena, is no longer alive, but his wife, Joy, still lives in suburban Chicago. She attended the same high school and an interview with her is imperative. She might remember what Bosh's life was like outside the baseball diamond and the classroom.

Bosh received dozens of athletic scholarship offers from around the nation. There was even speculation in the local press that he would go directly into professional baseball. He was that good. Ultimately, as we all know, he decided to attend college and selected Princeton University. Why Princeton? Einstein? Everett?

Princeton

Princeton changed his life. Before he could throw his first official pitch as a Tiger he injured his elbow in a preseason practice. His collegiate and professional baseball promise gone forever. Tellingly, there is nothing to indicate that this event had any negative impact on his personality. Did his baseball talent mean more to others than it did to him? Research his university friendships and interview those still alive.

His undergraduate years were, in a word, unremarkable. It was around this time that he came across the writings of Fernando Pessoa. Bosh credited Pessoa's concept of the heteronym with leading him to actively consider Everett and Many Worlds. Any biography must explore this link between art and physics. It also illustrates his life-long interest in philosophy and literature. (Another reason he was attracted to Elaine?) Bosh was toward the top of his class without distinguishing himself in any substantial way. His academic record, his contacts and his aptitude, however, were sufficient to earn him a place in the coveted post-graduate world of Princeton physics. After receiving his MA and authoring a largely uninspired thesis on quantum formalism, Bosh began his doctoral work. It is here that he publicly commits to Everett and Many Worlds. This period has been described as his 'born again' phase. Everything he does academically revolves around proving that the wavefunction does not collapse. His faith is unbreakable. In select scientific circles around campus he becomes known as 'the doctoral crackpot.' Night and day he wheedles his advisor, the venerable Dr. Milton L. Susskind, to allow him rein to pursue his ideas.

Many Worlds

And then we arrive at Bosh's *annus mirabilis*, the summit of his theoretical meditations and his personal life. In any narrative this should be positioned as both predictable and magical. Within fifteen months, Bosh writes his groundbreaking dissertation, battles with Susskind to see it published and meets and falls in love with his future wife, Elaine Mae Turing, a post-grad English student. At this point the biography, the story of Bosh, must divert into his revolutionary dissertation in tremendous detail (at least one substantial chapter sketching quantum theory history and explicating Bosh's enormous intellectual leap) without alienating general readers. Tricky. It would require a delicate touch to pull off, but is of supreme importance. It is the linchpin and the *raison d'etre* for the entire book.

Understanding the reception of the dissertation is also critical. The reader must get the sense that Bosh's ideas have turned the world of physics on its ear, that his work was revolutionary. This marks a turning point in support for String Theory. Guard against sensationalism and hyperbole, but do not understate the significance of both popular and critical receptions.

At this junction the book must acquaint the reader

with the backstory of Elaine Mae Turing: a brief summary of how she was raised, her interests, her personality, and her time at Princeton. They share the same Midwestern roots, love of literature, etc. Good transition to the Madison years.

Professional Physicist

Bosh is once again courted by institutions around the world. (Undoubtedly Bosh himself recognized that the process was eerily similar to his baseball recruitment.) Susskind lobbies Bosh to stay at Princeton. The generous freedom and responsibility offered by the University of Wisconsin convinces him to gamble on a comparative longshot. The Midwest connection certainly aided his decision. At a young age—Bosh is just over thirty years-old—he is cheerfully burdened (energized? challenged?) by the demands of creating a world class research institution basically from the ground up. Did he bite off more than he could chew? His passion for the project was recalled by almost everyone who knew him. He traveled the globe selling his ideas and his program. His recruitment—and some would say conversion—of the highly regarded Madeleine Tsou was the organizational highlight of those early research years at Chamberlin. See her brilliant autobiography for additional information.

Elaine settles in near her family and teaches literature at the university.

A Brief Family

As is so often the case, the most devastating falls are those from the greatest heights. Promising early success in the lab at UW (illustrate the technical issues in a general way without jargon) and, by all accounts, an idyllic home life were both short-lived. Jerome and

Elaine failed to create the family of which they dreamed. This led them to adoption. Report the tragic details of the death and failed adoption as dispassionately as possible, but imply that nothing was the same after the events. How could it be? Concurrent with the familial misfortune, Bosh suffers a major professional blow when the results of his first major experiment (articulate the issue and what was at stake in a clear and concise manner) were an unmitigated disaster. These dark experiences combine to drastically reduce his intellectual enthusiasm and his investigative drive. In many ways he begins to act like a broken man. He distances himself from his colleagues to devote more time and effort to his wife and marriage. The final blow—and this cannot be emphasized enough—was when his trusted colleague and confidant, Madeleine Tsou, announces that she is leaving to work for a rival team at Columbia in New York. It was as if he'd lost another family member. Again, reference the insightful and wonderful Tsou book.

The Dream Deferred

Bosh never really recovers from this series of events. The trifecta of the children (and the emotional impact on his wife), the poor test results and Madeleine's departure started him on a decline that would continue for the remainder of his life. To the outside world— apart from the tiny and insulated physics community— this shift, this slide was imperceptible. His fall (the metonym almost makes it sound biblical) was broken by sudden fame. On the evening of his fiftieth birthday, at a well-attended party in his honor, an unknown videographer captures what becomes one of the most discussed and viewed YouTube videos of all time. Be sure to include a moderately lengthy section on the videographer (Bernard Soares?) who went on to his own quasi-fame in the entertainment industry. The result is that Bosh feels his only choice is to embrace his celebrity. He resigns from his research position and becomes a more active teaching professor. He also becomes a hot commodity on talk shows and news broadcasts. In the truest sense of the word he becomes a celebrity. To those who knew him best, (see Elaine's emails) he never seemed comfortable in the role.

Discuss his effectiveness as a science celebrity and as a teaching professional. I cannot help but use my own recollections—after the fact, in the case of the video—of the man who became (whether he knew it or not) my mentor. Bosh once told the class that "we live microscopic lives with macroscopic minds." Be careful not to taint the overall message with personal reflection. Use my memory as lattice instead of foundation.

The Later Years

Although he remained a celebrity for the rest of his life, the public's interest in him waxed and waned with the passing years. He continued to teach with intermittent enthusiasm (see university HR records) until Elaine, the love of his life, was diagnosed with the cancer that would kill her, painfully but quickly. In many ways Bosh felt her death was the end of his own life. See Tsou quote. He was not far off. Shortly after his wife's death he was diagnosed with Alzheimer's and, as far as the rest of the world is concerned, was never heard from again. Unable to see to his own needs, his care was arranged by his sister and her husband, Jeffrey. At this point, without being too maudlin and acknowledging family sensitivity, include

143

the author's meetings with Bosh. During one of my visits, I remember thinking that senility, like childhood, is an old Heisenberg picture. It is a state, a condition, not a series of events. Nothing is connected. When we speak of senility and childhood, we speak of probabilities, of possibilities. The observed can either be measured or it can be placed, but not both. We can describe the event without contextualizing it or we can contextualize something without a description. Non-observance of the universe is impossible. We must always find ourselves alive and observing the universe in some form or another. I knew you were correct even then, Dr. Bosh, didn't I? Be sure to refer to our, usually one-sided, conversations shrouded and clouded by his horrific disease. In real terms, Dr. Jerome Owen Bosh was gone, only his ideas remained alive and they had never burned brighter.

The End?

One month before Dr. Jerome Bosh succumbed to the complications of Alzheimer's disease, Madeleine Tsou and the team at Columbia University made the breakthrough that Bosh had predicted all those years ago. (Remind the reader of the dissertation and the definitive test.) Bosh died unaware of the discovery.

Digress here to explain and reiterate what a momentous scientific breakthrough had occurred. Extrapolate the impact this has had on science, philosophy and humanity in general. It cannot be underestimated!

End the story, his story, with the funeral. It is an affair attended by many, particularly those who understood or appreciated his contributions to science and humanity. Describe the ceremony and the words of praise. A sister loses her only big brother. Include part of my speech from the eulogy. Wrap up loose ends. Madeleine Tsou awarded a Nobel Prize which she dedicates to Bosh, etc.

The final paragraph should convey the sense of hope his ideas have left us: something to the effect that somewhere in another parallel world, in a billion billion parallel worlds, Jerome Owen Bosh is alive, old but vigorous, standing tall on that dais in Stockholm accepting his well-deserved Nobel Prize. His healthy, loving wife Elaine beams with pride from the first row. He smiles back at her and waves. This happy (alternate?) conclusion summarizes the great man and his work.

Possible Titles?

Riding the Wavefunction: The Story of Jerome Bosh
The Many Worlds of Jerome Bosh
The Quantum Immortality of Jerome Bosh
Jerome Owen Bosh: The Probability of Winning a Nobel Prize
We Are All This and More: The Heteronymous Lives of Jerome Bosh

I have read and reread my notes, an admittedly skewed, brief sketch of the major events in your life, ten or eleven times. I've lost count. And you know what? I've come to the conclusion that I will not accept the honor of being your biographer. I don't think I can write your story. I don't think that I'd be able to do it justice. I don't think anyone else would either. To be quite honest, I don't want to reconstruct your life—your lives. Your life (all life, I suppose) is too variegated, too complex, and too special to fit between the cloth-wrapped cardboard covers of a book. I would be taking a position, an artificial academic viewpoint, purely for the sake of argument. I would not be capturing the man. I would not be revealing anything novel to the world. The book would be about me, not you. It would be how I see you. It wouldn't be you. It would take an infinite number of books in an infinite number of worlds to approximate the infinite fantastic lives of Jerome Owen Bosh. There is nothing of value I, or anyone else, could add. I would only be subtracting. I would be reducing, compressing, compromising. And that is not how I want to spend my time in this world. Nor, I believe, would it be a fitting tribute to you.

No, we all live many lives. More than we will ever know. And thanks to your insight we are certain that we are also living many other lives in many other worlds. As human beings it will take us a very long time to fully appreciate what this means. I imagine we will be struggling with it philosophically for centuries. Perhaps we've been struggling with it since the dawn of human thought. What does it mean to be me? The implications are overwhelming, the answer perpetually out of reach. I remember when I first read about the Many Worlds interpretation. The thought made me physically unsteady, wobbly. It's like that first time you gaze up at the nighttime sky and consider the countless visible and invisible stars and the vastness of the universe. Thanks to you, and many others, we've added incalculable, unseen universes to our understanding. We have come far. We keep getting smarter and smaller, don't we? I expect life will forever be more and less than we can imagine—a very quantum thought, isn't it? How could anyone hope to explain that in the pages of a single book?

Larry Francis is also the author of *Derrida's Toast* and *Halves*. He lives in France.